THE TOWER WITHOUT A DOOR

H. L. Macfarlane

4

Dedicated to the two Eevees in my life. You are both annoying and I love you.

PROLOGUE

Nobody liked the king much, and the people of Willow least of all. Golden-haired and handsome Pierre Saule was a war hero, though, and well-respected and intimidating enough that neighbouring countries did not wish to cross him. For that he had managed to cling to the throne for ten years, despite his cruel disregard for the common people he was supposed to rule.

In contrast his beautiful wife, Mariette, and his brother, Francis, were beloved by all. Francis tempered his older brother's bad behaviour by acting as the head of his council and, with the help of a powerful wizard who had served in Pierre's army for years, ensured that the country did not fall into ruins. Mariette worked with a team of loyal doctors to bring better health care to those too impoverished to pay for it, and spent more time on the road touring the country than she did in the royal city of Willow or the palace itself.

When she gave birth to a baby girl two years after Pierre had taken the throne, the kingdom rejoiced. With Mariette and Francis there to teach the child she was sure to become a better ruler than her father, the common folk said.

Over the next eight years the Princess Genevieve grew into a bright, intelligent and well-mannered young girl, whom even her father came to adore. She had his golden hair, and his green eyes, and thought that he could do no wrong. Perhaps it was a narcissistic kind of love on the king's part, but it was as close to true love as Mariette had known the man to be capable of.

For though the pair kept up a united front to the kingdom, behind closed doors the king and queen often argued. Mariette should spend more time in the palace, Pierre would say, even as his wife prepared for another tour of the country alongside Francis that would keep her away for two months. She would respond in kind – that it should be the king himself who joined her on the tour, not his brother – but Pierre would not listen. He didn't want to mingle with the common folk. In order to punish his wife he would refuse to let her take Genevieve along on her tours, though he knew he was hurting his daughter in the process, too.

Every night before Mariette left the palace she would comb her daughter's golden hair, singing soft lullabies and telling Genevieve how much she loved her. Genevieve longed for such nights with her mother; when she and her uncle were gone all she had was her father, who stayed in a perpetual bad mood when they were both away.

And then, on the eve of Genevieve's eighth birthday, the fragmented, fragile peace that had been so hard-fought for within the palace was broken. For Mariette and Francis had long-since been more than what they seemed, hiding their passion for each other from the king at every turn. But it had been common knowledge in every little town and village the two of them had visited; the people simply loved them enough to keep their secret. But eventually rumours began to spread to the wrong ears, and the king finally learned the full extent of what had been going on for years behind his back.

For it was not only the king who had golden hair and green eyes.

Furious and humiliated, and unable to look at the little girl he had always thought his own, Pierre had his wizard spirit Genevieve away to live out the rest of her days in the man's enchanted tower, without so much as an explanation to the princess about what was going on. He imprisoned his wife in the palace – a punishment only fitting for a woman who thrived on exploring the country. When he discovered that the wizard had long since known of her infidelity Pierre imprisoned him in the palace, too, upon pain of death of his eighteen year old son should he try to escape.

The king had planned to behead Francis for his treachery. He wanted nothing more than to watch his brother die, after all. But his pride was stronger, and he did not want his country to know just how humiliated he was. So, instead, Pierre banished his brother, ordering him to never set foot inside the country he loved so much ever again.

The king pretended to his kingdom that everything was fine, and informed the people that both Mariette and Genevieve had fallen ill, explaining their absence from the public eye. When eventually his wife was forced to bear him a son, Pierre rejoiced. He did not need his 'daughter', now that he had Prince Louis. His line and rule would continue as intended.

It was perhaps some ironic twist of fate that his young son grew up genuinely sickly. Even the king's wizard could do nothing for him. Everyone knew the boy was unlikely to reach adolescence, so time and again the wizard urged for Pierre to bring back Genevieve.

Yet the king's pride was too great. Genevieve was not his daughter. He would not give his brother the satisfaction of having his child sit upon the throne. Many times he tried to produce another heir but Mariette was too frail from her imprisonment to have another child.

11

Pierre did not want to marry again, or father a bastard, for doing so would involve having to admit to his country that there was a problem he could not solve on his own.

Eventually the king was forced to concede that bringing back Genevieve may be his only option. The girl did not know her father was, in fact, her uncle. Pierre could train her for the throne under the belief that she was still his. Genevieve had always adored him, after all. She was the only one who had.

And so he ordered his wizard to magic her back to the palace from his enchanted tower. Pierre would ensure his daughter trusted only him; not her mother. Everything would be fine. Nobody would ever know Genevieve had been locked away far from the palace for so long.

But something unexpected happened.

When the wizard cast the spell to bring the princess back, she didn't appear.

Genevieve was gone from the tower.

CHAPTER ONE

Genevieve

Today marked the end of Genevieve's twelfth solitary year, which coincided with her birthday. Twenty years since her birth, and more than half of those spent with nobody to touch or talk or listen to. She no longer wasted her time – though she had so much of it – wondering why she had been spirited away to the tower in which she now lived. For it was a pointless endeavour, as there were no answers to any of Genevieve's questions.

"What do you think we've been sent for breakfast today, Evie?" she asked aloud the moment she'd woken up and stretched her arms above her head. Genevieve

13

hands grabbed the rope from above her and yanked her back to the windowsill. She kept her eyes closed until the same pair of hands pulled her through the window and roughly threw her to the floor.

Evie's heart had been throbbing before; it was nothing compared to how painful it was now. She'd nearly died, and for what? Managing to climb down all of three feet from the tower window – two of which had only been achieved through falling?

It took Evie a few seconds before her brain finally kicked in and reminded her that someone had saved her life.

Someone. A person. A human being.

She flung her eyes open.

A man stood there, face covered in stubble with hair overgrown across his eyes. A ragged cloak hung from his shoulders, obscuring the rest of his tall frame. Though Evie couldn't see his face properly she had the overwhelming feeling that he was glaring at her.

She didn't speak. She didn't know what to say. All she could do was stare.

The man bent low to regard her. Evie, tangled in her hair and the rope and with muscles made of water, did not move away.

"Who," he began, disturbingly quietly, "are you?"

CHAPTER TWO

Julian

"I said – who are you?"

The young woman Julian had only just hauled through the tower window merely stared at him, unblinking.

Can't she speak? he wondered. *Or can she not understand me? Perhaps she has been instructed not to say anything.*

But then, after a few more moments of silence broken only by laboured breathing, the woman answered him. "Evie. Genevieve. Princess Genevieve."

Julian was too stunned to hear the 'Princess' part. He narrowed his eyes. "What were you doing trying to enter my tower?"

"I...what?"

"Why were you trying to get in here? What were you looking for? Who sent you?"

Genevieve stared at him in disbelief. "I was trying to *leave* the tower! So it's yours? Why have I been locked up in here for twelve years? What did I do?"

Oh.

Julian hadn't expected such an answer. Why would a young woman be trapped in the Thorne family tower? It didn't seem reasonable. It sounded like a lie. But Julian had been travelling for almost thirteen years, in an effort to stay as far away from home as possible.

Genevieve could be telling the truth.

He swept the hair currently obscuring his view away from his eyes and regarded her critically. Genevieve certainly didn't look like a spy. Her powder blue dress was finely made, but it was too short in the skirt which ended just above her knees. It was bordering on downright outrageous.

Perhaps she is a thief and stole the dress, which is why it doesn't fit, Julian supposed.

Yet the dress was not the most outlandish thing about

the scrawny young woman currently trying to inelegantly right herself from her position on the floor, for Genevieve's sun-coloured hair was longer than she was. When she finally stood Julian watched as it pooled by her feet like liquid gold. She regarded him with green eyes devoid of suspicion or fear, which given the situation she was in didn't make any sense.

Genevieve looked half-starved, though not in the gaunt, desperate way Julian had witnessed in the faces of many an impoverished village. No. There was...something else. The woman in front of him was hungry for something that wasn't just food.

She was, quite simply put, the most bizarre person he'd ever seen.

"Why should I believe that you've been trapped in here for so long?" Julian demanded, standing back up to his full height as Genevieve brushed herself off.

"Well, why should I believe that this is your tower?" she countered. "Twelve years here and I have not seen you once. I haven't seen anyone at all."

Julian's spirits fell just a little. He'd almost hoped his father would have somehow appeared in his son's absence, though of course that was impossible. His father was dead.

He rubbed at the furrows near-permanently creased into his brow. "Just suppose I hypothetically believe you.

24

Why have *you* specifically been locked in here?"

Genevieve looked at him as if he were stupid. Julian was taken aback, and a touch affronted. Nobody ever looked at him like that.

"I told you already," she said. "I'm Princess Genevieve."

"The princess and her brother have been sick for years. They are bound in the palace until they recover." Julian might have spent thirteen years avoiding Willow but that didn't mean he was ignorant of the goings-on in the royal city.

Genevieve dropped the long, make-shift rope she'd just begun untying from one of the old, rickety bed posts. It landed on the gnarled wooden floorboards with a dull thump. Her eyes seemed altogether too bright; Julian almost looked away from them, her expression was so intense.

"I have a brother? I have -"

"Louis," he elaborated for her benefit. Whether Genevieve really was the princess or not, Julian knew that the conversation would only move along if he gave her all the information she craved. "He's eight, I think. So why have you been locked up here all this time?"

She didn't seem to hear him. Instead Genevieve jumped back over to the window and sat on the sill. "A brother. A baby brother. And my mother? My father?"

25

"Excuse me?"

"Are they alive?" Genevieve asked without looking at him. The fact she was ignoring his questions in favour of barraging him with her own annoyed Julian to no end.

"Yes," he replied, fighting to keep his tone polite. "But Queen Mariette has also taken ill. Nobody knows with what, though. She hasn't been seen away from the palace grounds in years."

Genevieve absorbed this information in silence.

Julian supposed that she looked enough like King Pierre to be his daughter, what with her golden hair and green eyes, and she was of an age with the princess. But that wasn't proof enough of *being* the princess. Genevieve could have been lying about being trapped in the tower for so long. She might simply be insane.

He turned from her, inspecting the room his father had so often retired to in order to read and practice magic. Julian had never liked the tower much, preferring instead to stay at home in their handsome, well-made house on the outskirts of Willow with his mother. That was, until she died. After that Julian had spent just as much time in the tower as his father had until the man mysteriously disappeared.

Julian liked the tower even less now, years later. Though, looking closer, he had to admit that the solitary room inside it did indeed look lived in. Perhaps

Genevieve was telling the truth.

"You're a wizard...right? Can you get me out of here?"

Julian was so lost in his head that he didn't hear her questions at first. But then he turned to the so-called princess, who was now watching him instead of the window with a hopeful expression on her face.

He nodded, thinking that the sooner he got Genevieve off his hands then the sooner he could sleep for three days straight and figure out what to do with the rest of his life, now that he was home once more.

"I'm a wizard, yes."

"Hence the poofing in out of nowhere," Genevieve said, excitement colouring her voice. Julian didn't like the ardent way she was looking at him at all, so he turned his face away from hers.

"I'll send you to Willow, but not to the palace. I don't want to get arrested. You can seek an audience with the king yourself."

Genevieve clucked her tongue unhappily. "I didn't mean – I don't want to be spirited off to Willow. I just want you to send me down there." She pointed to the meadow at the base of the tower. "I've been stuck here for so long. I'd prefer to travel to Willow on foot."

Julian laughed before he could stop himself. It was

cruel, he knew, but he didn't care. "You? Walk to Willow? Have you seen what you're wearing, little girl, or the state of your hair? Do you have any supplies? Money? Do you know how long it would take to reach the city? Do you even know the way?"

"I...no," she admitted, with some hesitation. But then Genevieve shook her head, stood up from the windowsill and smiled brightly at Julian.

Oh, lord, no.

"You could take me!" she babbled excitedly. "I mean, this is *your* tower. Don't you want to know why I've been locked up in here all this time?"

"No."

"And you could update me on what's been going on in the country the past twelve years," Genevieve continued on, as if she hadn't heard Julian. "And then, when I reach the palace, my father will reward you handsomely for helping me find my way back home, and then –"

"I said *no*," Julian cut in, louder this time.

Genevieve frowned. "But why not? Do you not pity me for being locked up? Are you so callous a man that you would not help a person in need?"

"Absolutely."

Neither of them said anything, though Genevieve's

cheeks puffed out as if she was holding back from yelling profanities. He wondered if she even knew any, given that she must have been a child when she was first locked up.

Julian glanced at the window. "Last chance for me to send you straight to Willow, *princess*."

"I shall walk," she said, resolutely ignoring his jibe, "if you would be so kind as to point me in the right direction."

I should just send her to Willow regardless, Julian thought as he reluctantly joined Genevieve by the window. He pointed east, through the forest. "That way," he murmured. "Stick to the outskirts of the woods as best you can and you'll reach a small town by nightfall. From there you can find someone to give you better directions to Willow."

Genevieve didn't reply. She stared in the direction Julian was pointing, frowning slightly against the sun. A small spray of freckles crossed the bridge of her nose, he noticed. He began joining them together in his head, forming constellations, when Genevieve turned her attention from the forest to Julian himself.

"What's your name?"

"I don't have to tell you that."

"No, you don't, but it would be nice if you did."

God, she's annoying, Julian thought, though he reasoned there was no harm in giving her his first name.

"...Julian," he finally answered.

Genevieve inclined her head politely. "Thank you for saving my life, Julian, and thank you in advance for releasing me from your tower."

"Don't die on the road," Julian said, unsmiling, before raising his left hand and clicking his fingers. And just like that Genevieve was gone, only for her to reappear down in the meadow, several paces away from the tower.

She looked up at Julian in awe; her golden hair caught the breeze and blew behind her like a cloak. "That felt so strange!" she exclaimed. "Thank you!"

"Go away!" he yelled back, then turned from the window to investigate the rope Genevieve had presumably constructed to escape. It was surprisingly well made. If she'd been a little stronger – better fed, with muscles given a chance to develop properly – Genevieve likely would have made it to the meadow unharmed.

But Julian didn't want to think about her any more. All he wanted to do was sleep.

Several hours later he lay awake and uncomfortable on a bed that smelled completely different from when he had last used it thirteen years ago. It smelled of the 'princess', he knew. The entire room did. He couldn't escape it.

But Genevieve was no longer Julian's problem. It was up to somebody else to help her now. So why couldn't he stop thinking about her?

"She wasn't wearing any shoes," he muttered, reluctantly rolling out of bed to pack a bag before he could stop himself. "Who doesn't own shoes?"

CHAPTER THREE

Genevieve

"Yes, just let a young woman walk barefoot into the woods," Evie muttered, though in truth she was too excited to be all that angry with the wizard who'd – reluctantly – helped her.

For how could Evie allow negative feelings to befoul her mood when she was beneath the boughs of an old oak tree for the first time in her life? Even when she'd lived in the palace, or ventured into Willow, she'd never stood under such a gigantic tree.

But soon the soft, spongy grass beneath Evie's feet would turn to pine needles and sharp twigs and stinging weeds. They would make quick work of her soft, unblemished flesh, she knew.

If only she had shoes.

Julian told her to avoid wandering deeply into the woods, so Evie hoped the ground wouldn't get too uncomfortable to walk on. And then, when she reached the town he'd told her about, she could finally buy a pair of shoes that fit.

"With what money?" Evie asked aloud, stopping in her tracks as if floored by the question. But of course she needed money; it was hardly as if she could announce herself as the Princess Genevieve and expect the town to help her out. After all, she was fairly certain Julian did not believe she was the princess, and he had far more reason to believe her than an unknown town would.

He should have given me some money, at least, Evie grumbled, though in truth that wasn't fair. Julian had offered to magic her all the way to Willow – she had brought the problem of money and shoes and shelter upon herself. But she had to live with her decision to recklessly walk herself to the royal city, so with a sigh Evie continued on her journey.

*

"Ouch!" she exclaimed after several hours of walking. It was not the first time she'd made such a proclamation, and it wasn't simply because of her aching, bleeding feet.

33

For Evie's hair kept getting caught on branches and roots and snagging painfully; eventually she was forced to carry her hair in her arms to avoid catching it on anything.

Now that it was past noon Evie had to admit her mood had decidedly taken a turn for the worse. Her stomach grumbled insistently, and she knew little and less about which plants in the forest were edible. Her hands were chafed raw from the number of times she'd had to catch the rough bark of a tree trunk to stop herself from falling when she stumbled.

And the sun. Despite the fact Evie was beneath the trees it still beat down on her through the canopy, pricking her skin with unbearable heat. There was a sheen of sweat all over her which Evie was desperate to wash away. And she was so thirsty, too. Once she acknowledged her thirst it was all she could think about, until her mind was so busy daydreaming about water that Evie tripped over an exposed tree root and fell flat on her face.

"This is ridiculous!" she decried, spitting out a mouthful of dried earth and leaves in the process. She crawled over to the tree whose root had upended her and collapsed with her back against it, then closed her eyes to the dappled sunlight. For a while all Evie did was run her fingers along the tree's roots as her chest heaved with exhaustion.

"I can't do this," she murmured, thinking of her failed

attempt to escape from the tower. If Julian hadn't shown up when he had done then Evie would have died.

Her stomach lurched unpleasantly at the mere thought of the tetchy, unkempt wizard. Even when Julian had pushed some of his dark hair out of his eyes Evie had not gained all that much more insight into his appearance. It left her feeling unsatisfied, that he should have seen her lying on the floor like a crazed fool, whilst Evie saw so little of the first human she'd had contact with for twelve years.

Julian was not a nice man, Evie decided. He had called her 'little girl' and refused to give her even the most basic of supplies.

"And he wasn't curious about why I was in his tower at all!" Evie complained, crossing her arms over her chest to emphasise her mood. "If I'd discovered a princess locked in my own tower then I'd want to know why she was there."

In truth Evie just as badly wanted to ask Julian questions about his own life. She'd had nobody but herself to talk to for so long, after all. And he was a wizard, and clearly connected to what happened to her on her eighth birthday.

"Well you'll never see him again, so just forget about him," Evie said, before brushing off her now filthy knees and clambering to her feet. She winced as they took her weight, and wondered how she could possibly keep going. And then she heard it.

Water.

A stream! Evie thought, delighted, and all complaints about her aching, bruised and bloodied feet were forgotten in favour of chasing the beautiful sound of water over pebbles. It took her a while to find it, for within the forest the sounds of the water echoed and reverberated in some places and were absorbed by moss and close-knit trees in others. By the time Evie finally felt moisture beneath her feet the trees overhead had changed from broad-leaved to evergreen, and there was no more sunlight filtering down to the forest floor.

But Evie did not care. Just a few minutes later she stumbled across the stream itself, though it was narrow and insubstantial. Another few minutes of impatient walking later and the stream grew wider and deeper. She stepped into the shallows and sighed contentedly. The bracing water soothed her feet and tickled at her ankles. Bending low she scooped some of it up and brought it to her parched lips, eagerly lapping at the water until she had her fill.

After that Evie was still hungry, but at least her thirst was sated. She decided there was no harm in following the stream for a little while longer, since it was still mid-afternoon. She had plenty of daylight left to find the nearest town, and now that she'd rested for a few moments and drank her feet no longer seemed so sore.

It was therefore to her surprise when, after about an hour of following the silvery path of the stream, Evie found what appeared to be a road. It was reasonably well-maintained considering it carved its way through the middle of a forest, so she began to follow it. Above her the afternoon sun beat down on her back, though soon it would dip beneath the trees as evening crept upon the woods.

"Why didn't Julian tell me about the road?" Evie wondered, once more annoyed at the wizard. "It would have made my journey so much easier." She could only assume he'd told her to walk beneath the trees on the outskirts to make her journey longer and more irritable in response to Evie having refused his offer of going directly to Willow.

"So petty," she grumbled, before making her way along the road in the general direction of east. Evie fashioned conversations that she might have when she reached the town as she walked. She knew they were unrealistic, and probably unhelpful, but they helped to pass the time as the sun lowered in the sky.

"Why yes, kind sir, I do indeed look like I've been locked up for years, but that would be because I have. Thank you for noticing. Would it be at all possible to spend the night in your inn?"

"Unfortunately this is the only piece of clothing I possess, madam. Might I trouble you to spare me even

37

the simplest of clothes?"

"As you can see I am not wearing shoes and have suffered for it. I would appreciate any help you can give me in procuring a pair."

But Evie was distracted from her ramblings when she heard the sound of several people laughing not too far ahead of her on the road. She was reaching a bend that promised to lead to the exit of the forest and the town ahead, which was likely obscuring the source of the voices from her.

What do I do? Evie worried. *Do I go ahead and try to catch up with them? Or do I stay back and wait for them to go?*

Her meeting with Julian had been disastrous, after all. Though Evie had spent her entire journey excited to talk to other people, now the very thought daunted her. She looked down at her arms, laden with her hair as if it were a babe.

I look weird and suspicious, I suppose. If they don't ignore me they will likely tease me. But it wasn't as if Evie could make herself look more presentable when she reached the town, so what did it matter if some strangers on the road saw her?

Then she realised the voices were getting louder and more boisterous. The group was heading her way and unless Evie hid beneath the trees she would meet them.

She took a deep breath, figuring that it was better late than never that she saw people who weren't bad-tempered wizards like Julian. For all she knew the strangers would take pity on her and help her.

So Evie continued purposefully along just as the sun began to set the tips of the trees aglow. She reached the bend in the road at the same time the strangers did – a group of five men who looked to be about as old as Evie remembered her father being, though they looked far less elegant and refined than he had been.

Their cheeks were ruddy; two of them were holding bottles of what Evie was fairly certain was wine, though perhaps it was something stronger. It wasn't as if she had any personal experience with alcohol given that she was locked away at eight years old.

One of the men cocked an eyebrow when they spied her. "And what have we here?" he said, slurring his words slightly.

So they won't ignore me, then, Evie thought. She held her arms as close to her chest as possible even though they were full of her long, tangled hair. She didn't know if she should speak or not. Would the men take offence if she didn't talk to them?

A second man took a step towards her and looked her up and down. "You're injured, my lovely. Would you like some help?"

Though the question was a nice one, the man's tone and expression were not. Evie flinched back; the group of strangers laughed.

"You scared her, Jack! No point in scaring her. She might run off."

"She won't be running anywhere in the state she's in," Jack replied, indicating towards Evie's feet. "What happened, little girl? Were you attacked and robbed?"

This time they waited for Evie to reply. Yet her voice was caught in her throat and wouldn't come out. She had never been scared of people before. But now...

When the man named Jack lurched forwards to grab her Evie yelped and stumbled away. The men only snickered harder.

"So she *does* have some life left in her," the first man said, a horrible gleam in his eyes as he circled around Evie. "That's good for us, then."

"P-please leave me alone," she stuttered, as all around her the group closed in and blocked off her escape. When someone grabbed her hair and yanked her to the ground she cried out in pain.

Evie struggled to get back to her feet even as Jack pushed her down once more. "Alf, keep hold of her hair!" he ordered the man who'd pulled Evie down in the first place. He grinned at her, showing Evie all of his dirty, yellowing teeth. "It shouldn't be difficult when she has so much. Have you never cut your hair, girlie?"

Evie merely wriggled beneath him. "Let me go! Let me go! Let me –"

"I'd like you better if you stayed silent."

"Ah, same here, but that doesn't mean I'd go to such lengths to shut her up."

Evie froze – as did the group of men. For it was not one of them who had spoken.

It was Julian.

Evie twisted her head until she caught sight of the scraggly wizard. His lips were contorted into a snarl, and his eyes – entirely free of hair for the first time – were glowing with anger.

No, not with anger. They were literally glowing, like burning, red-hot coals.

"Now, if you'd be so kind as to let my idiotic companion go," Julian said, "then I might not be inclined to burn all five of you to ashes."

CHAPTER FOUR

Julian

Julian was furious for several reasons.

First: that Genevieve had bothered him enough into actually packing a bag full of supplies to go out looking for her.

Two: that when he'd sent out a spell to find her location in the outskirts of the forest, he'd instead discovered that she was on the road, which was infamous for its thieves and brigands.

Three: that he had not warned her of said thieves and brigands.

And four: that the aforementioned brigands had found Genevieve and would have done any number of unspeakable things to her, had Julian not arrived just in time.

He was largely mad with himself, of course. Julian could have prevented all of this had he ignored Genevieve's ridiculous wish to walk to the royal palace and had magicked her there, instead.

But he didn't want to acknowledge his self-directed anger, when five wonderfully deserving targets for his fury stood in front of him.

The man closest to Genevieve had sneered at Julian when he'd first appeared, though he'd recoiled at the sight of Julian's eyes. He didn't *have* to make them glow. It was a pointless waste of magic, really. But it scared people who had little knowledge of spells and alchemy, and if the sight of burning eyes was enough to send the brigands on their way then Julian would actually *save* magic.

Burning five men to ashes took a lot of power, after all.

"I won't warn you again," Julian said, voice loud and commanding and imbued with the very real threat of fire magic. He took a step towards the group, avoiding making eye contact with Genevieve. He didn't think he could take any more of her terrified face than he'd first seen when he found her, struggling against the men

43

holding her down.

Two of the group stumbled backwards, but did not leave. The other three stayed where they were, and drew out several filthy-looking knives.

"You think you can scare us with your parlour tricks, wizard?" one of them said as he brandished his weapon.

Julian waved his hand in front of him and the man's blade shattered into pieces. Then his shirt began to smoke and smoulder, which he promptly threw off as he yelped in pain.

"That will be your skin next time," Julian said as the man attempted to stamp out the fire that was beginning to engulf his shirt. "So tell me: is it really worth your lives to see how much of my magic consists of *parlour tricks*?"

And yet still two of the men did not back down. Julian glanced at Genevieve before he could stop himself; she was watching him with unabashed awe in her eyes. It made him uncomfortable, so he looked away before she could realise his gaze had been on her.

"I don't think you have it in you to burn us," one of the men said, "or else you'd have done it already."

Julian shrugged his shoulders. "I suppose that could be true. It could also mean that I don't want to waste precious magic on people such as you. But you've irked me enough to push me into action." He sighed. "Good bye, gentlemen."

The men barely had the opportunity to draw breath into their lungs to scream before Julian clicked his fingers. But he did not set them alight.

He stunned them.

One by one they dropped to the ground with heavy thumps. The man closest to Genevieve fell on top of her; Julian expected her to push him off. When she did not he grew concerned and closed the gap between them.

He had accidentally stunned her into unconsciousness, too.

"Oops," he murmured, though a smile curled his lips. There would be no idle chatter to bother him as he took her to the nearest town, which suited him just fine.

Julian unceremoniously pushed Genevieve's would-be rapist and potential murderer to the side and then, upon seeing the state of her legs and arms and feet, swept her into his arms. She barely weighed a thing compared to the heavy bag across his back, though her hair was irksome.

"Why have you never cut it, you fool?" Julian wondered aloud as he picked the bulk of Genevieve's hair up and placed it all in her lap. He'd have to rectify the length of her hair himself, it seemed, once they reached an inn.

Julian could have transported the two of them straight there but something gave him pause. He didn't

45

know what. But it was still light enough in the summer twilight to finish the route to the nearest town on foot, and Genevieve weighed barely more than a tall child, so even though it seemed like madness Julian chose to walk the rest of the way.

Now I sound like her, he thought, looking down at Genevieve passed out in his arms. *Walking. Why would a wizard walk anywhere?* Now that the young woman was still and quiet Julian could see that she really *was* a young woman, despite her weight and childish demeanour.

If she gained some weight she might even be pretty.

Julian quickly pushed the unwanted thought away. Genevieve was already more trouble than she was worth; he had saved her life not once but twice in the space of a single day. He dreaded to think what tomorrow would bring.

"Ugh, tomorrow," he muttered, hating himself even more for coming to the aid of the woman in his arms.

Then Julian heard the sound of footsteps and froze.

"Who goes there?" he demanded, putting on his commanding, magical voice once more. The air sizzled with the power of his words, warming Genevieve's skin and putting some colour back into her gaunt, exhausted cheeks.

When a man crept out of the forest Julian was fully prepared to stun him like the others. But then he held up his hands in surrender and smiled.

"Just a regular traveller," he said. "I was spooked by all the noise I heard, so I hid in the trees. Didn't want any trouble. Is the little miss okay?"

Julian didn't reply, instead squeezing Genevieve a little closer to his chest before he could stop himself. He looked the man up and down – in the twilight Julian could make out blonde hair going grey at the temples, light coloured eyes and skin wrinkled with middle age. He was wearing well-made but plain clothing, and carried two bags over his shoulders. There was a sword on his hip.

A merchant, perhaps, Julian thought. *Or an ageing sellsword. Either way he is none of my concern.*

When Julian moved to walk past him the man cried out, "You're not going to harm her, are you?"

"Of course not!" Julian spat out. "What do you take me for, old man?"

"A wizard, I suppose. A powerful one. That girl in your arms would stand not a chance against you."

"I will not harm her," Julian said, when he noticed his potential foe had his hand on the hilt of his sword. "I mean to take her back to her family."

An odd look crossed the man's face, and Julian felt himself frown. There was something...off. Something uncanny.

"Do I know you?" he asked.

The man shook his head. "I would think I'd remember such a foreboding wizard. Anyway, I shall take up no more of your time. Take care of the girl for me."

And then he was off before Julian could ask any further questions. He stayed stuck to the spot, too baffled to move, until he felt Genevieve beginning to shift in his arms.

He sighed. There was no way he could cope with another hour of walking with her conscious. And talking.

"Magic it is, then," Julian said, and with a snap of his fingers they were gone.

CHAPTER FIVE

Genevieve

Evie regained full consciousness with a start, though her brain had been trying to claw its way back for a while before that.

"Where am I?" she demanded, swinging into an upright position in an unfamiliar bed in an unfamiliar room. Two lanterns were lit, casting a warm glow across sparse furniture and off-white walls. Curtains were drawn over the window, so Evie could not tell what time it was.

And then her stomach growled painfully, bending her over double.

"Fix that," a gruff voice muttered, followed by a small loaf of bread hitting Evie on her temple. "There's soup on the table."

She spied Julian sitting on a chair in the darkest corner of the room, glowering at her. To her left there really *was* a bowl of soup sitting on a small bedside table, so Evie picked it up with both hands and revelled in its warmth.

"Thank you," she tried to say, though it came out as more of a croak. Noticing a pitcher also sitting on the table along with a cup, Evie put down her bowl in order to pour herself some water. She drank the lot down so quickly that it took her a beat too long to realise the liquid wasn't, in fact, what she had assumed it was. Coughing and spluttering, Evie held a hand to her throat and tried to rub away the burning the liquid had caused.

In the corner Julian was cackling with laughter. "Serves you right for not looking at what you were drinking, little girl."

"I am *not* a little girl," Evie protested around another cough. "I'm twenty years old today. What is this vile stuff?"

Julian frowned slightly. "It's wine. Have you never had wine before?"

She shook her head. "I've been locked up for twelve years, remember? The last time I had *soup* was before that."

"What have you been living on, then?"

"Bread, mostly," Evie replied, picking up the loaf Julian had thrown at her. "Cheese. Apples. Sometimes dried meat. Water to drink. That's about it."

"No wonder you're so skinny," he said, casting his invisible gaze across Evie. Julian's eyes were once more covered by his dark, overlong hair. It annoyed her, but she didn't say anything. The wizard had saved her life twice today, after all. It would not harm her to show him some manners, though he seemed disinclined to extend the same respect to her.

Evie ate in silence for a while, during which time Julian got up and left the room. When he returned he was carrying a pitcher that *actually* contained water, left it by Evie's bedside, then took the half-full pitcher of wine over with him to the chair.

Julian took a long draught of the stuff. "Let me know when you begin to feel light-headed. I'll put you to sleep when you do; I don't imagine your tolerance for alcohol is particularly high."

"I don't want you to put me to sleep again!" Evie exclaimed.

"Ah, I didn't mean to, before. I got carried away."

The side-eye she gave Julian implied she definitely

didn't believe him. The man finished off his cup of wine, poured another and then moved over to sit on the end of Evie's bed. She put down her finished bowl of soup on the table and inched away from him.

He grimaced. "I just wanted to check that you're okay."

"I'm fine, thank you."

Julian arched an eyebrow. "Are you sure? You were covered in cuts and bruises when I found you. Your feet at the very least can't be in the best of states."

Evie felt a twinge of pain lancing down her leg even as he spoke. The dull ache of her feet crept up her nerves in earnest, telling her that Julian was correct. She looked down at her hands. "I guess I'm not feeling great."

A pause. Julian gulped down more wine before saying, "I told you to stay to the outskirts of the woods. It was the *one thing* I told you to do. Why did you ignore me?"

"I thought you told me that just to inconvenience me!" she replied, bristling. "You weren't exactly very nice to me, Julian."

He shook his head in disbelief. "Why in the world would I have done such a thing? I saved your life when you were hanging out of the tower, or don't you remember? Just because I wanted you gone didn't mean

I wanted you to take one step outside and immediately walk into trouble."

Evie said nothing. She knew she had acted brashly, and immaturely. If she had been not so naïve about the world around her then perhaps she'd have been more inclined to take Julian's directions to the town more seriously.

"Did those men – did they do anything to you?"

"No," Evie replied quietly. She looked away from Julian. She didn't want to think about the strangers on the road; it was too frightening to dwell on what they would have done had Julian not come to her rescue. "They pulled on my hair and bruised me when I fell, but that's all."

She ran her fingers through her hair as she spoke, wincing when she met tugs and tangles along the way. It was a mess. It would take her many painful hours to clean and untangle it all.

"Right, that's it," Julian announced, before putting down his wine and closing the gap between them. "I'm cutting your hair."

"Don't you – don't you dare!" Evie cried, squirming out of the way when Julian attempted to grab hold of it. He slung an arm around her waist instead, hauling her back to his side.

"What's so important about bloody *hair* that you

would let it become so cumbersome?!" he yelled.

"There was nothing to cut it with in the tower!"

"So let me cut it for you now!"

"No!"

"You brat, stop squirming and –"

"Stop yelling in my ear! Let me go!"

As soon as Julian realised he had pinned Evie to the bed he let her go and recoiled away. Evie's face was flushed. She was beginning to feel light-headed, which she put down to the wine. And her dress was in disarray, barely covering her at all. If she didn't have so childish a figure she'd probably have been embarrassed.

Julian ran a hand through his own hair and clenched his teeth in frustration. Now that Evie could see his face clearly she realised he was younger than she'd originally thought; he was perhaps only ten or so years older than her. By the way he spoke to her Evie would have assumed he was closer to fifty.

He glared at her. "What is honestly *so important* about your damn hair, little girl?"

"Stop calling me that," Evie replied, deliberately ignoring Julian's actual question. She didn't want to tell him about her memories of her mother brushing her hair and sending her off to sleep – those were hers and hers alone. In a world where Evie had so little, her memories were more precious to her than anything.

It seemed to Evie as if Julian knew she was deflecting. "Calling you what?" he asked, as if he didn't know exactly what he'd just called her.

Evie rolled her eyes. "Little girl. Brat. I told you; I'm not a child."

"So, what, should I call you *Princess*?" he asked scathingly.

"Just call me Evie."

"I thought your name was Genevieve?"

"It's too long. Call me Evie."

"*Fine...*Evie." Her stomach flipped upon hearing Julian call her by the nickname she'd given herself. She didn't like that at all. When he glanced at her Evie realised his eyes were blue. "If you won't let me cut your hair then at least allow me to do *something* about the state it's in," he insisted. "It will only get worse on our way to Willow."

Evie's spirits lifted, all previous unpleasant feelings forgotten immediately. She drew herself up onto her knees. "You're coming with me?! You're actually going to show me the way?"

"Don't make me regret this before we've even begun," Julian said, sliding a hand over his face in obvious exasperation. "Something tells me you would still refuse me magicking you to the city despite what happened in the forest, so I have no choice but to accompany you."

She nodded at the wizard's observation. "What would *you* want to do if you'd been locked up for twelve years, Julian? Would you not want to explore the world before returning home and maybe getting answers to your questions that...you might not like?"

Julian stared at her, baffled. "You're more astute than I thought."

Evie laughed bitterly, though she hated the sound. "How many times do I have to tell you that I'm not a child? I know that my return to the palace may not be what I hope it will be. But still I have to hope, otherwise what's the point?"

He sighed, then motioned for Evie to turn around. Obediently she did so, though she flinched when she felt Julian's hands pulling her hair away from her; it had tucked itself beneath her legs in their fight on the bed.

"I'm not going to cut it, I swear," he muttered. He brought his fingers to her scalp, massaging them into the roots of her hair with surprising gentleness. "I'm just going to work some magic."

Evie's heart lit up at the prospect. "You're giving me magic hair?"

"Don't be ridiculous. I'm simply working magic

upon it. Now be silent, and be still."

Evie's skin tingled as Julian worked on his spell. She was faintly aware of the fact her hair was lit around its edges in a fiery way akin to Julian's previously glowing eyes. It sent a shiver down her spine, to think of him full of furious magic and ready to kill someone at a moment's notice.

"I told you not to move," he complained.

"I can't help it!" Evie protested. "Your magic tickles!"

Julian made a noise of disgust at the comment, but then he put his hands on Evie's shoulders and roughly pushed her off the bed towards a mirror hanging on the wall. Evie hadn't seen her reflection in anything larger than a cup of water for twelve years; she was nervous to see what she looked like.

But she didn't even notice her body, nor her face – not at first, anyway. She only had eyes for her hair.

Julian had cleaned and untangled every last golden strand of it, and had woven it into so intricate a braid that Evie couldn't tell how and where it started. The style brought her hair off the floor, the end of the braid only just skimming her ankles, which was far more practical for walking and running and just about anything else Evie could think of.

"Julian, this is –"

"Don't you dare thank me," he muttered, before heading for the door. "I did that for my own benefit, else I'll end up having to carry you to Willow just so you don't trip up over your damn hair. We leave immediately after sunrise."

And then he slammed the door and was gone, leaving Evie to stand in front of the mirror alone.

In contrast to her glorious, shining hair, the rest of her was underwhelming. Evie's skin was sickly pale, and there were shadows beneath her eyes. The bones of her elbows jutted out too much, and her cheekbones were too prominent. There were barely any signs that she had an adult woman's body, though Evie remembered her mother's figure had been invitingly curvy. She longed for the rest of her to match her hair – to look as beautiful as her mother and father.

"Guess I need to eat more," Evie decided, returning to the bedside table to retrieve the half-eaten loaf of bread from earlier. "I want to look my best when I return to the palace."

For there was nothing else Evie could control about the situation, and she knew it. She didn't like it one bit.

Perhaps it was because of the wine in her system, or the fact that she had a full stomach for the first time in years, but that night Evie fell asleep so quickly she might have been inclined to believe Julian had put a spell on her.

Maybe he really had.

CHAPTER SIX

Julian

"How long does it take to get to Willow on foot?"

"Ten days, as the crow flies."

"But we are not crows."

"I am aware, Evie."

"So how long will it take?"

"Longer if you keep asking me."

When Evie came to a halt on the gravelled road in a huff it was all Julian could do not to yell in frustration.

She crossed her arms over her chest, the elaborate braid Julian had woven into her hair swinging behind her like a pendulum. "Why can't you just tell me the answer instead of making fun of me?"

"*Fine.* It will take about four or five weeks, as I wish to stop by several towns on the way. Lord help me survive so long in your company. Are you satisfied now?"

"Very," Evie grinned, unfolding her arms and skipping on ahead of Julian in barely-concealed delight. He had a growing suspicion that Evie wanted the journey to Willow to take as long as feasibly possible, despite the fact she was eager to reunite with her family.

But she was aware that she may not get the welcoming she desires when she arrives, Julian mused. *For all we know it was her parents who sent her away in the first place.*

Julian had to force himself to keep walking instead of freezing to the spot. He was thinking as if he truly believed Evie was, indeed, the princess. But what evidence had she provided to support this? Other than having blonde hair and green eyes – traits not as rare as they once were a generation or two ago – there was nothing about Evie that suggested she was royalty.

She was polite and well-spoken, Julian supposed, but any girl of reasonable birth would sound like her. And she had not yet talked of her life before the age of eight – such as when she deliberately dodged Julian's question about her hair – which either suggested Evie was lying about being a princess or didn't want to talk to Julian about her childhood.

Which is bizarre because she won't shut up about everything else.

He watched Evie bound even further ahead of him like a collie dog. He'd bought her a brown cotton dress with a white undershirt from the innkeeper's wife, whose adolescent daughter had outgrown them. Despite the fact Evie was twenty – which Julian still struggled to believe – the clothes fit her much better than her previous dress had, though she refused to throw that one away. He also procured her a pair of boy's trousers and a lace-up shirt as a change of clothes, as they were the only other garments he could find to buy.

Lastly, he'd made Evie a pair of shoes. Well, they'd been his and he'd enchanted them to perfectly fit her feet. Clothes Julian could cope with not being a precise fit on Evie; shoes he could not. If her shoes were too big or too small then she would complain about it and he would suffer a migraine for the duration of the journey to Willow.

Genevieve didn't look too bad now that she'd been cleaned up and clothed in something that fit her, though Julian wondered if she merely looked better because of her hair. He had to admit that he'd probably used more magic on it that was strictly warranted – he certainly hadn't needed to fix it in such an intricate hairstyle – but it looked so beautiful he scarcely cared. For as long as Julian could remember he'd been using magic for practical purposes only, to hone and enhance his offensive, defensive and enchantment skills. To use it for purely aesthetic reasons (though admittedly the underlying spell to keep Evie's hair out of the way was a useful one) was a rarity for him.

But now Evie's hair was a work of art. The innkeeper's wife had been in awe of it that very morning, and many of the early-rising townspeople had stared at her as they left. It left Julian feeling distinctly proud of his work, though he'd never say as much out loud.

Evie, however, had grown self-conscious. "They will think I'm not pretty enough for such hair," she'd admitted, very quietly. If Julian had been a nicer, more patient person he'd have comforted her. As it was, he disliked early mornings and had instead snapped at her to finish eating breakfast as quickly as possible.

The girl had eaten like a piglet, though Julian could hardly blame her. If Evie had truly been stuck in the tower eating nothing but bread and cheese then of course she was ravenous. He made a mental note to stock up on extra food in every town; he had a feeling she'd devour it all.

"You know, you wanted to cut my hair even though your own desperately needs a trim," Evie said, breaking a blessed ten minutes of silence. Julian wondered if that was the longest stretch of peace and quiet he'd get over the next month.

"My hair doesn't trail on the floor though, does it?" he countered, darting out of the way when Evie reached up to try and touch it. "Even if I let it grow for twelve years it wouldn't be as long as yours."

"Is it not annoying to tie it up? I'll admit it's an improvement over letting it hang over your eyes, though."

Julian scratched the side of his temple. He wasn't used to having all of his hair tied back in a knot, but it made sense. He had to keep on high alert during the journey if he wasn't simply going to transport them using magic, so keeping his eyes clear was a necessity. But now everything seemed too bright, and he had to make eye contact with people, and he hated it.

"And are you not boiling to death inside that cloak?" Evie remarked, fingering the fraying edges of the material. "At least buy yourself one that isn't so damaged –"

"Are you quite done with criticising my appearance, *Princess*?" Julian asked through gritted teeth.

Evie said nothing. She merely stared at him expectantly until he gave in and answered her question.

He sighed. "I'm used to concealing myself from other people," he finally explained. "As a wizard, it's not a good idea to let someone see if you have a particular solution or spell or weapon on you. And you don't want them to know if you have injuries. And you don't want other wizards and spell-wielders to use any old scars or defining features to their advantage. Better to keep it all hidden, even if it *is* uncomfortably hot beneath a cloak in summer."

The answer would have satisfied the average person. Evie was not average.

"What do you mean by other spell-wielders?"

"Magicians," Julian said, making a left off the rood to cut through a small strip of woodland to a stream. He needed to refill his water skin to combat the scorching heat of the midday sun. "Alchemists. Doctors."

"Doctors are spell-wielders? What's the difference between a magician and a wizard?"

He crouched low beside the narrow, gurgling stream and dunked his container into the water. It wasn't as cool as Julian would have wanted, given the heat of the day, but it would have to do. "What doctors can achieve these days is practically akin to magic, one might argue," he murmured. "Some of them know just as much – if not more – than an alchemist or experienced herbalist knows about the properties of poisons and mind-altering substances."

"And magicians?"

"Generally wizards are born with an affinity for magic whereas for magicians it's far more of a learned skill. They also mostly deal with curses and transformative magic instead of combative and defensive spells, for the most part, though admittedly the line between magicians and wizards is becoming blurred."

Evie paused to consider this. "You transformed my shoes and enchanted my hair. Does that not make you a magician?"

"And now you see my point," Julian said, standing upright once his water skin was filled and stretching his shoulder muscles until they cracked. "One day the two words will likely become entirely synonymous. But I'm far better versed in combative magic than the average magician. Or average wizard, truth be told."

"Was the magic you used on those men combative?"

He nodded. "Or defensive, as the case may be. Stunning them did no harm – it merely allowed us to escape."

I must surely have given her enough to think about for the time being, Julian thought as they picked their way back to the road through the trees. Evie jumped up and grabbed a couple of apples from a low-hanging bough; she threw one to him before happily biting into her own.

"I can't fathom how you're still hungry," Julian mused. "You ate enough for three people at breakfast and we're only an hour out from the next inn for lunch."

Evie shrugged. "You might have noticed I could do with gaining a little weight. And when will I ever have an opportunity to be a glutton like this again?"

"You *are* aware that I'm the one paying for your food, yes?"

"And when we reach the palace I shall have my father repay you for every meal. You *are* aware that he's the king, yes?"

"So you keep reminding me," Julian mused, before taking a tentative bite of the bright red fruit Evie had tossed him. It was deliciously sweet, though he personally preferred the sharper, green variety. He glanced at her out of the corner of his eye. "You haven't told me anything about your childhood, Evie."

"I know."

"Why not? It would lend some credit to your story."

To Julian's surprise, Evie chuckled. It wasn't her usual, childlike laugh; it was an altogether more adult sound. When she turned her head to smile at him with her woven, golden hair framing her face and the sun turning her irises to emeralds, Julian saw glimpses of a woman who really *could* be King Pierre's daughter.

"Because I have no reason to tell you," Evie said, "just as you have no reason to tell me about you. Or were you expecting me to spill every secret from my childhood when you so clearly do not wish to divulge anything about that tower of yours, or why you were absent from it for so long?"

Julian didn't reply.

Evie was right, and it infuriated him to no end to admit it.

CHAPTER SEVEN

Genevieve

Over a week had passed since Genevieve had nearly died trying to escape Julian's tower. In that time she had annoyed the man so much that he'd been driven to bark at her to shut up on no fewer than nine separate occasions, though Evie rarely heeded his demand for longer than half an hour.

And yet despite how often she spoke she still refrained from telling Julian anything substantial about her life before being trapped in the tower. Sometimes Evie wondered if that was irritating him more than her never shutting up; other times she was fairly certain it was the incessant talking driving him insane.

Either way, Evie was revelling in finally having company – even if Julian was quiet, angry, tired and bored most of the time.

"What do you think of – Evie, for the love of god, we just had lunch!"

Evie had picked up a pastry from a market stall, paid the vendor and already taken a large bite from the delicious baked good before Julian had noticed what she was doing. She grinned bashfully.

"Sorry," she said around mouthfuls of buttery pastry and sweet raspberry jam. "I was still hungry."

Julian raised his face to the sky and closed his eyes. Evie was familiar with the gesture; he did it when the two of them were around other people and he wanted to resist shouting. "I told you not to make me regret giving you money to buy things."

"But you shouldn't regret me eating, Julian!"

"It's a perfectly acceptable regret," he countered. "At this rate we'll run out of money barely halfway to Willow."

Evie stuck her tongue out. "I know you have most of your coins hidden somewhere in your cloak and bag. There's no way we'll run out of money before we reach the palace."

Just as Julian was about to retort the vendor who'd sold Evie the pastry burst out laughing. The pair of them turned to the woman, surprised and confused.

"Don't the two of you make such a funny couple!" she said. "And your hair is so beautiful, miss. Do you braid it yourself? Or does your lovely companion do it for you?"

Evie pulled Julian away before he could begin spouting angry protestations about being mistaken for a couple, all the while trying to smile at the woman with her pastry firmly between her teeth.

"Why did you do that?" he demanded, before ripping half of Evie's pastry from her mouth and unceremoniously shoving it into his own. She glared at him for half a moment then continued consuming what he had left her. "All I was going to say to that woman was that she was mistaken; why would I ever be together with a skinny, brattish, annoying –"

"You're going to have to find another word for 'annoying', Julian," Evie said mildly. "It's getting awfully boring." This was not the first time the pair of them had been mistaken for a couple, after all; considering they were a man and a woman travelling together it was only natural for the towns and villages they passed through to assume as much.

Evie didn't mind being viewed as a woman in love, wandering the country with her partner. Even *if* the

71

partner was a tetchy wizard who somehow never got enough sleep to satisfy him, though he insisted on getting up at daybreak. It certainly beat staying in a tower all by herself.

"I think 'annoying' works just fine," Julian replied, before directing Evie down the market street to a green-and-gold shop front. "I want to go in here. Can I trust you to stay out here and not cause any trouble? Or will I have to magic your mouth shut and tether you to the door?"

She swatted his arm. "I can behave. Why can't I just come in with you?"

"Because my business is my own."

"Typical."

"Says the woman who talks at length about nothing but stays silent on anything meaningful."

"...fine," Evie conceded, before crossing her arms and leaning against the shop front. "But don't keep me out here for long or I really *will* misbehave."

Julian's eyes glittered at the pseudo-threat, almost on the cusp of glowing with magic. Both he and Genevieve knew fine well she would not do anything of the sort. She said such things to rile him up and, to Julian's dismay, it usually worked.

He needs to do something about his temper, Evie

thought as Julian wordlessly left her side to enter the shop, a bell above the door chiming prettily when he did so. She shifted on the spot, trying to readjust her arms across her chest to make herself more comfortable.

The clothes Julian had bought her merely a week ago were beginning to grow tight. Evie liked the feeling of it, for it was proof that she was finally gaining weight, but in another few days they would likely become unwearable.

She glanced down at her chest. Every night, when she was left alone in her room in whichever inn Julian had picked for them to stay in, Evie would look at herself in the mirror and wonder if she was any closer to looking as grown up as her mother did. She supposed it *was* working – her hips and her breasts were certainly curvier than they had been a week ago, and Evie's face no longer looked gaunt and underfed. But it wasn't enough.

She wanted her body to match her beautiful, golden hair. The magic Julian had worked upon it was quickly becoming both a blessing and a curse to her.

"I was never so narcissistic back in the tower," she grumbled, "though it's hardly as if I knew what I looked like, either."

Out of the corner of her eye she noticed than several passers-by were glancing at her, some of them more than once. Her hair really *did* stand out, what with its length and colour and intricate, weaving hairstyle. Julian's magic repelled dirt and grease from it, and kept her hair from

73

forming flyaways and tangles, so Evie hadn't unravelled the braid even once. It meant it looked perfect at all times.

Unlike the rest of me.

"No, Scarlett, I am *not* getting involved with that."

"But Adrian –"

"Absolutely not. There's just...far too much drama involved with something like that."

Evie tried not to make it obvious that she was watching the unusual couple bickering a few metres away. They were possibly the most beautiful people she'd ever seen. The man's jet-black hair was broken by a solitary white streak, and there was a single hanging emerald adorning one of his ears that matched his green waistcoat. He looked the epitome of a charming gentleman...except for his amber eyes, which had a predatory edge to them that reminded Evie of the wolves her mother used to tell her about before bed.

The woman also had black hair, though it was thick and wavy and tumbled over her shoulders. She wore a deep red dress so finely made that many of the female townspeople sighed with longing as they passed her. Her face was pale and fair, with the hint of a smile on her lips that suggested she knew a secret nobody else was privy to.

I think they might be even odder than me and Julian,

Evie decided, just as the wizard himself exited the shop and returned to her side.

He frowned at the couple she was watching. "Who are they?" he asked, immediately suspicious. He held a small bag in his hands from the shop, though he slid it into the folds of his cloak before Evie could ask what he'd bought.

She shrugged. "I don't know. I think they might have been talking about us, though."

"How do you know?"

"Just a hunch. They're going in the opposite direction to us, anyway. It probably doesn't matter."

Julian didn't look satisfied with Evie's answer but he took it nonetheless. "Come on," he said, "we still have hours of travelling to go before we reach our stop for the night."

"Why don't you dress like the orange-eyed man back there?" Evie asked after a while. "You might actually look good."

Julian clucked his tongue. "Hardly one of my top concerns, Evie."

"Don't you want to find a wife?"

He didn't reply; his silence spoke volumes.

That would be a no, then.

"Do *you* want a husband?" Julian countered, much to Evie's surprise. "When you return to the palace and take up your place as princess, I mean. You'll probably have to."

"I hadn't really thought about it seriously," she admitted. "I guess marriage is still an abstract concept to me."

"Better to keep it that way," he mumbled, so quietly that Genevieve almost missed it. She chose not to reply; it was a subject she realised she'd rather not discuss.

That afternoon they travelled together in uncharacteristic, awkward silence for the first time.

Evie didn't know why it bothered her so much.

CHAPTER EIGHT

Julian

It was just before midnight and Julian couldn't sleep. Normally he collapsed into bed the moment he reached an inn – walking all day was exhausting, and Evie's incessant chatter even more so.

Except for today. He and Evie hadn't spoken since the marketplace in the previous town, which Julian didn't understand. Had she stopped talking to him because he'd asked her about whether she wanted to get married?

It can't be that, surely, he thought. *Evie said herself she hadn't even considered the idea all that much. That it had been a hypothetical situation, since she reasonably assumed she would never get to leave the tower.*

But then why had she stopped talking? Julian had felt so awkward in the silence yet he couldn't find the words to break it. And Evie had a faraway look plastered to her face, as if she wouldn't have heard anything Julian said even if he *had* spoken.

With a sigh he lurched out of bed, slid on his boots and headed towards the inn's tavern, thinking that perhaps some ale would ease him into unconsciousness. He hesitated for a moment when he passed Evie's room, running his fingers along the grain of the wooden door as he did so. He wondered if she was asleep, or whether he should ask if she wished to join him.

The thought almost made Julian laugh. *Here I am with a perfect opportunity to be alone and I'm considering deliberately asking Genevieve if she wants to annoy me? Ridiculous.*

And so Julian left her door and continued downstairs. There were a mere handful of men still sitting in the tavern, though the ones at the bar respectfully kept their distance from him when he walked up to it. Even without his cloak on, and wearing a simple white shirt and trousers, Julian exuded an aura that told people to stay away. That he was unusual. That he was powerful. He supposed that was his magic's doing.

It never keeps Evie away, Julian mused as he ordered a tankard of ale. *It's like she doesn't know or care about it, or cannot feel it.*

"Fancy seeing you here, wizard."

He turned; several stools away sat an oddly familiar figure. When he moved over to sit by Julian he recognised him as the man who'd hidden on the road when Evie was attacked.

Julian frowned. "I thought you were travelling in the opposite direction from me?" he asked. "How did you end up here?"

The man's shaggy, greying blonde hair shook as he laughed. Julian realised that maybe it really *was* time to cut his hair, or at least tidy it up – the stranger looked half–mad.

"I'm not heading towards any particular destination," the man replied. "Haven't had one for a while now. I just go where I feel like going."

"I can relate to that," Julian said, thinking of the past thirteen years of his life. Looking back he felt like most of it had been a waste – he had no standout memories from his period travelling abroad. No notable people to drastically affect his course in life; no stories to tell of monsters felled and villages saved; no sweeping, epic romances that would likely make Evie blush. All Julian had done was improve upon his magic, which he could have done anywhere.

I may as well have been trapped in a tower all alone.

As if reading his mind, the man asked, "How's the girl? Did you get her home?"

Julian nearly told him that Evie was still with him on reflex, but remembered to be suspicious at the last second. "I did," he said, narrowing his eyes as he took a long draught of ale. "Glad to be rid of her."

"That's not very nice, wizard. I'm sure she was quite lovely."

"And how could you be so sure of that?"

He shrugged. "A hunch."

Julian realised he'd been right to be suspicious; the stranger clearly knew far more than he was letting on. Julian could not be sure for what purpose he was interested in Evie, so he downed his ale, nodded at the man and promptly left the tavern. He didn't want to say something that gave the stranger more information that he already had, after all.

I'll have to keep a closer eye on the road, Julian thought as he crept up the stairs and passed Evie's room. *I don't want to be followed or –*

A thump came from behind Evie's door. Julian froze in front of it, wondering what had caused the noise. Just as he concluded that it was probably no more harmful than the young woman falling out of bed in her sleep – Julian snickered at the thought – he heard Evie stifle a sob.

He slammed the door open to check on her before he could stop to think things through. Evie *was* on the floor, both blankets and her long, long hair twisted around her legs and waist like serpents. But there was nothing amusing about her having fallen from her bed.

Evie's face was ashen, eyes glazed over in horror as she sobbed and sobbed.

Julian didn't know what to do. He knew he couldn't stay standing there merely watching Evie, either, so he closed the door behind him and took several tentative steps towards the young woman on the floor, though Evie didn't seem to realise Julian was there.

"Evie?" he asked, voice a little uncertain. He bent down by her side and reached out a hand to check her temperature; Evie recoiled from it with such force that her head thumped against the wall.

"You fool!" Julian exclaimed before he could stop himself. This time he bodily picked Evie up despite her trying to wriggle away and placed her back in bed. He pinched her pale, tear-stained cheek. "Wake up already. Wake up. What happened?"

Evie blinked several times and looked down at her trapped limbs. Wordlessly Julian set to work untangling her; she trembled beneath his fingers. *I've never seen her so scared,* he thought. *Not even when she was hanging out of the tower was she this afraid.*

81

"Evie, what happened?" Julian asked again, forcing his voice to be altogether far gentler than it had been the first time.

She shook her head miserably. "It was just a dream. A nightmare. I'm fine."

"Clearly not. Tell me what happened."

When Evie sat up against the headboard and drew her knees to her chest Julian chose to sit beside her. Usually being in such close proximity to Evie resulted in him wanting to scream at her or throw something in annoyance, but not now. Julian felt an overwhelming urge to protect the small, shivering woman in front of him, whose impossibly long hair was beginning to unravel around her face.

I need to put some magic back into her hair, Julian noted as he reached a hand out to tuck a lock of it behind Evie's ear. She watched him do so with wide, unguarded eyes.

"Why do you care so much about a nightmare, Julian?" she asked. Her voice was barely audible.

"If a woman who I know to be fearless enough to climb out of a tower window using a rope made of clothes can be reduced to *this* after a dream," Julian said, waving a hand in Evie's general direction, "then of course I care. What did you see that was so bad?"

Evie didn't look at his face. She sighed, then wrapped

her arms around her knees. "I was back in the tower."

"That doesn't seem all that bad."

"It was surrounded by thorns," she continued, as if Julian had never interjected. "They were everywhere. Black and twisting and sharp. They grew in through the window and trapped me where I lay. I couldn't escape them. They cut into my skin, and then they cut deeper. It was like being suffocated; I could only watch them close in on me as they slowly killed me. It was..."

Evie didn't finish her final sentence. It didn't matter which word she used to describe what happened – horrifying, frightening, terrible – it clearly would not do the experience any justice.

Julian felt an uncomfortable finger of ice creep down his spine. That Evie had dreamed of thorns unsettled him deeply. But he hadn't told her his surname, so there was no explaining away her dream as subliminal based on things she'd heard.

It can't be prophetic, Julian thought. Evie had displayed no signs of magical talent so far. *But can a mere 'bad dream' really be bad enough to send her into such a panic?*

"You think it's stupid," Evie mumbled into her knees. "You think *I'm* stupid."

"You and I both know I don't think that," he chastised. "Just because you're insufferable and

83

oftentimes an idiot doesn't mean you're stupid."

Julian was pleasantly surprised when Evie laughed at the remark. He smiled slightly. "If you're feeling better then I'm going to head back through to my -"

"No, don't go!" Julian stared down at his sleeve; Evie had grabbed it before he'd even had the opportunity to stand up. Her fingers clenched through the material down to his skin, promising fingertip-shaped bruises in the morning if Evie didn't let go soon.

He raised an eyebrow. "Where do you propose I sleep, then? On the floor? Because I'm not doing that."

"Sleep in the bed with me," Evie said. There was absolutely no trace of an ulterior motive on her face - but then again, there never was. "Please," she added on, when it became clear Julian was going to decline. "Please stay."

The two of them stared at each other for a long time, Julian frowning and thinking whilst Evie's green eyes were bright and pleading. Another lock of hair fell across her face; when Julian reached forward to place it behind her ear he knew he wouldn't leave.

"Fine," he sighed, exasperated. He hauled off his boots and lay down beside a victorious Evie. "You win. This is a one-time thing, though. I don't much revel in the idea of squeezing onto a narrow bed with a skinny brat for company."

Evie swatted his face; this close together she barely had to reach her hand out to do so. "I'm not so skinny now. And I'm not a brat."

"You really are. Look what you're having me do! All because of a nightmare. You're such a child."

When Evie smiled at him Julian could help but breathe an inward sigh of relief. Things were back to normal between the two of them after their awkward afternoon of silence, which Julian was glad for despite his preference for quiet.

"Good night, Julian," Evie said before snuggling into the crook of his arm.

"Don't you dare fall asleep there!" he complained, though Evie had already laced her hand through his to bring it over her shoulder. Julian could have kicked himself for giving into her ridiculous request, but when Evie's breathing slowed and she fell back into a far more restful slumber than before he forgot to be annoyed.

Just once, he thought. *I can indulge her just once.*

There was a growing problem, however. This close together Julian realised something about Evie he'd have rather not had to deal with. For Evie was right: she wasn't a brat. She was a woman.

And Julian's body was reacting to that even as he screamed at it not to.

This was going to be a long, awful night.

CHAPTER NINE

Genevieve

It was just before dawn and Genevieve was wide awake. She had slept comfortably for a few hours after waking from her nightmare, but the feeling that she wasn't alone in her bed was quick to rouse her when the room began to lighten.

Julian, Evie thought, too cowardly to turn and see his sleeping face behind her. *I can't believe I asked him to share a bed with me. I can't believe he* accepted *my request to share a bed with me.*

It seemed like madness that she'd asked him to spend the night with her. But Evie hadn't really expected

Julian to agree to keep her company – she was just an idiotic child reacting badly to a nightmare, after all.

Although he said I wasn't stupid. He was almost kind to me.

Evie didn't know what to do now that she was awake. The bed was narrow and Julian was tall. There was barely enough space for him on it – let alone Evie, too. It meant she was pressed up against him, her legs interlaced with his.

A furious blush began to creep up Evie's neck. *I only have an underdress on and it's currently bunched around my thighs!* But Evie didn't dare reach down to fix her clothes; she didn't wish to risk waking Julian up. His soft breathing tickled Evie's head, sending errant strands of hair wafting over her face.

The magic's come undone, she thought, picking up a lock of golden hair and inspecting it for signs of having been stuck in a braid for a week. But there was not a single crimp or crease or wave to it – Evie's hair was as straight as if she'd kept it unbound and free instead of tied up.

She huffed out a small breath of air. *Magic is so strange. Where does it come from? How did Julian learn to be a wizard? Was he just born this way? He* did *say wizards tended to be born with an affinity for magic.*

With every passing day Evie longed to learn more

about him, despite the fact she was wary of telling Julian anything about herself. At this point she wasn't sure why she was keeping her childhood secret; Evie trusted the wizard, after all. For how could she not? Julian had saved her life twice, then chosen to help Evie travel to Willow on foot, and now he was even comforting her when she had bad dreams.

Don't dwell on the dream, she thought, though it was difficult not to. It had been so vivid – so alarming – that when Evie had awoken all she could see around her were thorns. They'd threatened to overcome her; to entrap her; to control her. They represented everything Evie had tried to escape from, the moment she'd decided to climb out of the window of Julian's tower.

She squeezed her thighs together in discomfort only to remember, too late, that one of Julian's legs was between them. Evie's previous blush grew bolder. She was thankful the wizard was far more clothed than she was, otherwise things would probably have been much worse.

This is still the most indecent I've ever seen him, though, Evie thought. She craned her neck around in order to try and peek at Julian without disturbing him. But he was fast asleep, so Evie risked slowly sliding her legs away from his to turn and face him.

In stark contrast to what he looked like when conscious, Julian's face was serene as he slept. Without a scowl on his face he looked younger, once more reminding Evie that he really couldn't be much more than a decade older than her. Although, given their current situation, she sincerely wished she *hadn't* thought about such a thing.

Stop it, Evie, she scolded even as she held the fingertips of her right hand millimetres from Julian's face. But she couldn't help it; she wanted to know if she could feel...something. Anything. A sign that Julian held the power to set things on fire – to just as easily stun a group of men as he could enchant a young lady's hair. She wanted to feel that buzz of magic that made her heart sing when his blue eyes began to glow like molten glass.

Then Evie tried to see past the magic she was longing to feel. Beneath it, Julian was a tired man desperately in need of a shave, a haircut and some new clothes. In that respect he was not so dissimilar to Evie herself.

He's really strong, Evie mused, casting her gaze along the line of Julian's shoulder and down his arm. He'd carried her onto the bed the night before as if she'd weighed nothing at all. *And that's not to mention how easily he pulled me back into the tower when I was falling!* But hidden beneath his cloak Evie had never seen whether Julian actually had the frame to support such strength, or whether he'd used magic to help out every time.

Now she knew. Despite the fact Julian always

appeared to be old and tired and unkempt and resigned he was, in fact, a perfectly healthy man who was probably stronger than most even *without* magic.

And he is handsome, I suppose, Evie thought despite herself. *Though it's not as if he seems to care about his looks all that much. When you're a powerful wizard I guess it doesn't matter if women fawn over you for your blue eyes or not.*

It made Evie hate her own growing narcissism. Did she honestly care so much about becoming beautiful like her parents? Was that really all she had going for her? She was a *princess.* Beautiful or not she would have opportunities abound once she returned to Willow and the royal palace.

Her stomach lurched at the thought, so Evie turned from Julian and closed her eyes as if doing so would somehow eliminate all her doubts. But they lingered, ruining the warmth of the sun as it crept over the horizon and ventured through the window into the room.

Just what was waiting for Evie when she returned to her parents? Would they be glad to see her? Or would they be angry? Why was she sent to the tower in the first place? What could the eight-year-old Princess Genevieve have possibly done to warrant such a cold, cruel punishment?

And why was it *Julian's* tower?

"Shh," Julian mumbled against her ear, clearly still fast asleep. Evie hadn't said anything out loud; she had to wonder if Julian's power extended into being able to read her mind. She didn't like that idea one bit.

Perhaps he is dreaming of telling me to shut up, since he has to do it so often when awake, she thought, which was a far more appealing explanation. Evie almost giggled at the idea of her annoying the wizard even in his sleep, but then Julian slung an arm over her waist and pulled her in against him and all such amusing thoughts were lost.

Evie's eyes darted downward to Julian's hand, which rested on her stomach. For there was the thrum of magic she had longed to feel earlier, pinning her in place against him. It wasn't uncomfortable; rather, the peculiar sensation was almost pleasant. Like Julian was keeping her safe.

But he's doing it in his sleep, she thought. *Does he know he's doing it? Just how powerful is he?*

As if in protest to Evie's brain running through a million questions at once Julian squeezed her against him just a little tighter, and her mind cleared. For soon the wizard would wake up, and then he'd go back to being his usual, dour self. Evie would likely not get an opportunity to spend time with him like this again.

I guess I should make it count, she thought, before snuggling against Julian's side in much the same manner as she had done when he'd first agreed to share her bed. But things were somehow different than they had been hours before, in the dead of night. Evie felt altogether like she was growing up at a rate far faster than she had done when she was alone in the tower. Sleeping beside a grown man she was not married to was not something she was supposed to do...especially not when her thoughts towards said man were beginning to verge on impure.

But Evie was content to push such troubles off onto another day, along with everything else she had to worry about. The morning sun, and Julian's soft breathing, and the knowledge that she was free from the tower, was enough to satisfy her.

For now.

CHAPTER TEN

Julian

Ten days had passed since Evie's nightmare and, just like that, the pair of them were more than halfway through their journey to Willow. Julian should have felt relieved. Soon he'd be able to wash his hands of the young woman beginning to encroach on all his thoughts and he could go back to his unremarkable life of trying to improve his magic for a goal he could never reach. There was just one problem.

Julian was beginning to wish his journey with Evie *wouldn't* end.

It wasn't that she had suddenly become less annoying

or less exhausting to look after. No, everything was pretty much the same as it had been from the very beginning. But the closer they got to Willow the more Julian felt like they were being followed, and the more he became aware that perhaps there was something from Evie's childhood that would tell him why.

Given how reluctant Evie was to tell him anything, despite all that they'd been through so far, Julian concluded that whatever it was wasn't going to be pleasant, and that the two of them really would be better off never going near the royal palace.

"How is your hair a mess *again*?" Julian complained when he spied Evie return from a market stall in the town they were passing through, arms laden with a heavy basket full of food. "I only enchanted it five days ago." Her golden hair was coming undone around her face; with her dishevelled dress and rosy cheeks Evie looked decidedly as if she'd taken a tumble through a meadow with a young lover.

Except that's just what she looks like all the time because she has absolutely no self-awareness, Julian thought, grabbing the basket of food from Evie's arms so that she could tuck her hair behind her ears.

She smiled bashfully. "I guess my hair is as greedy as I am. It must love your magic quite a lot."

He snorted in amusement at the comment. At least Evie was honest about her insatiable appetite. "Sounds about right. I think you need more clothes."

"I *know* I need more clothes." She looked away and blushed as she spoke, which at first confused Julian. But then he noticed the way some of the local boys were looking at her, eyeing the way her breasts were just a little too visible above the neckline of her dress, and how the curve of her hips brought the hem of her skirt above her knees.

The dress I found *her in fits her better than this one now,* Julian thought, before unceremoniously handing Evie the basket of food to carry once more simply to cover her chest. It wasn't just that she looked indecent in such an ill-fitting dress – it was that the pair of them travelling together when Evie looked like that made *Julian* feel indecent, too. Had he really been so blind to Evie's situation that he was only realising the discomfort she must be feeling now, almost three weeks after they'd first set off on their journey?

Out of the corner of his eye a flash of movement caught Julian's attention. Just a hint of someone sliding between two market stalls, but it was enough for him to know that he and Evie were definitely being followed through the town.

He rummaged inside his cloak and fished out several gold coins before sliding them into the basket Evie was holding. He bent low towards her ear, then pointed down a side street. "Buy yourself something that fits better from

96

there. I'd say buy *several* things that fit you but you seen intent on tripling in size by the time we reach Willow, so there's no point."

Evie smiled softly at the comment, though it didn't reach her eyes. She glanced at Julian a little uncertainly. "What's going on, Julian?"

"Just do as you're told. Please," he added on, when it seemed as if Evie was going to protest. Instead she merely stared at Julian long and hard; he resorted to finding constellations in her freckles just as he had done the first day he'd met her. The sun had brought them out over the last three weeks; they were much easier to see now. But Evie didn't budge even as Julian continued to stay silent.

Then he pulled a gold coin out from behind her ear, like a common street magician, and she burst out laughing. "Okay, okay, I'm going," Evie said, waving back at Julian before heading in the direction he'd pointed out. He watched her walk away with a smile on his face, though when he spied the same boys as before leering at her it quickly turned into a scowl.

He sent out a thread of magic towards them – not enough for the boys to notice, but strong enough that Julian could keep track of wherever they went whilst he searched out whoever was following him. If they got too close to Evie he would know; the magic in her hair made certain of that. On more than one occasion Julian had wondered whether he should tell her that part of the enchantment he'd cast on her was a tracking spell, though ultimately he'd decided against it.

Nobody wanted to know they were being watched. Followed. Under constant supervision.

Least of all Julian himself.

It didn't take Julian long to work out where his and Evie's stalker was hiding. He crept along one side street, and then another, and finally down a dark, hidden alleyway blocked off by a large market stall selling trinkets and vases. When he spied a shadowy figure leaning against a rough stone wall Julian recognised him immediately.

"You," he spat out, sending fiery magic down to his fingertips in order to light the alleyway in front of him. For the stalker was no other than the greying, middle-aged man whom Julian had met on the road the day he'd saved Evie's life, then in the tavern a week later before her nightmare. "I should have known."

The man smiled humourlessly. "You *did* know, wizard. You simply hadn't done anything about me following you yet."

"Give me one good reason not to blast your head from your shoulders," Julian demanded, taking another step forwards and sending enough magic to his fingers that the air began to crackle and spark around them. He was satisfied to see the man flinch back from it all.

"You're strong," he said. "Very strong."

"Are you hoping to compliment me into letting you go?"

"Not at all. I'm merely glad that the person protecting Genevieve is more than up to the task."

Julian froze; his magic faltered. "How do you know her name?"

The man's eyes darted around as if looking for someone. "You *are* being followed, you know. Not just by me."

"I'm aware. How do you know Evie's name?" Julian repeated, his tone altogether more demanding this time.

To his surprise, the man's serious expression broke for a moment. When his eyes lit up Julian took a moment to realise they were green.

"Evie," he said. "Mariette would love to know she goes by that. My brother didn't like it, though, so she never went by Evie in the palace."

Julian's brain was working overtime to try and connect the dots, much like he did with Evie's freckles. *She's really the princess?* he thought despite himself. All this time Julian had only half-believed her. Evie could just as easily have been driven insane from being stuck in the tower for years, or from hitting her head, or –

"You are surprised to learn that the woman you're with is Princess Genevieve."

It wasn't a question.

Julian shook his head, dismayed by his own lack of knowledge. "Not surprised. Merely..."

"You thought she was lying about it?"

"How much do you know, stranger?" Julian asked, frowning. He returned a little magic to his fingers, for all the good it would do. "Have you been listening to our conversations?"

"Only in the beginning," the man admitted. "I had to be sure I could trust you to keep her safe, so I listened to everything."

Julian didn't like this at all. He hadn't known they were being followed in the beginning.

"You don't need to look so upset," the stranger laughed. "I've learned a thing or two about cloaking myself from a wizard's eyes."

"So I only became aware of you following us because you wished it to be so?"

He nodded. "I'd hoped you'd have more time to move Genevieve to a place far from here by now, but that hasn't been the case, so..."

"You don't want Evie to go home?"

The man laughed incredulously. "Do you not recognise me yet, Julian?"

He paused. "Should I?"

"Aside from my physical similarity to the king, and my knowledge of Genevieve's upbringing, the fact I was the one who convinced your father to work on the grand council after the war was over should have informed you of who I was."

"But that was..." Julian's voice trailed away as he thought back to his childhood. "I was a boy then. Only eight. I thought it was the king who came to see my father directly."

"Pierre hates to travel. He sent his brother in his stead."

Oh.

"You're Francis Saule."

"In the flesh."

Julian's eyes narrowed. He returned his hand to his side, snuffing out the magic within it in the process. "You were exiled. For –"

"For a lie," Francis interrupted. He snorted. "Well, my dear brother lied to the country, that is. He made me out to be a war criminal. In truth what I did was far worse...to him, anyway."

"Speak plainly or not at all," Julian said. The thread he'd sent out after the local boys was beginning to tug, warning him that they were far too close to Evie.

Francis' eyes were hard. "I hurt his pride."

"That doesn't explain a damn thing and you know it."

"It should," he said. "You must know how proud our dear king is."

"I've spent the last thirteen years travelling, twelve of which have been spent avoiding dealing with my father's death." Julian had never been so honest – with a stranger, no less – about his father. But this man, the king's brother, had known Jacques Thorne. He might have been a stranger to Julian but he was not to his father.

Francis' smile was sad and genuine. "Perhaps it's for the best you haven't been around to witness the king's character. I'm sure he would ensnare you for your powers had you stayed close to Willow."

Julian ignored this. Nobody was going to trap him, least of all the king. He never intended to work for anybody he had not chosen to help himself. "What did you do that hurt your brother's pride so much that he exiled you?" he asked.

"I fell in love with his wife."

Oh no.

"And she fell in love with me."

Please stop.

"I fathered a daughter the king always believed to be his."

He isn't stopping, Julian thought, dismayed. He wanted to cover his ears with his hands – to block out all the drama and betrayal he had accidentally walked right into, the moment he'd saved Genevieve's life.

"Genevieve was sent to your father's tower to live in isolation," Francis continued, as if he took no notice of Julian's distraught expression. "She was never told why. My brother...he loved her, in his own way. He couldn't stand to look at her after he found out her true parentage. The fact he's looking for her now must mean he's aware she's no longer in the tower. He –"

"Wait," Julian said, holding out a hand as he attempted to take in Francis' deluge of information. "Just wait. The king had Evie – the princess – sent to my father's tower. Why? Why, specifically, Thorne tower?"

Francis shook his head sadly. "Because he worked for my brother, and was the most powerful wizard he had at his disposal."

There was something about the man's explanation that didn't feel right. Julian wanted to press him for further answers but the thread of magic connecting him to the boys lurking after Evie pulled against him more insistently than ever. She was leaving the shop, and they were there, waiting for her. Julian had to get her first.

"Don't let her reach the palace," Francis said, reading Julian's intention to leave the alleyway from his face. "Pierre *can't* get hold of her. Stay off the roads. Keep her safe."

"You lost the right to tell Evie what to do the moment you allowed the king to trap her in a tower," Julian uttered, so angry on her behalf that his eyes began to glow. He turned from the king's brother, stalking back through the throng of the marketplace until he found Evie standing nervously by the entryway to the tailor's shop.

She beamed when she saw Julian, evidently relieved to no longer be on her own. "Julian, what do you think of –"

"We're leaving," he muttered, grabbing Evie's arm and pulling her away from the predatory stares of the boys lingering nearby.

"Julian, what's wrong with –"

"Nothing. We just have to leave."

But everything was wrong with Julian. Evie really was the Princess Genevieve, and the king had really banished her to Thorne tower. Julian's *father* had been involved, somehow, and shortly thereafter he'd disappeared and died.

He was missing some vital pieces to the puzzle, and he had no idea how to find them. There was only one thing Julian knew for certain.

There was nobody either himself or Evie could trust except each other, and nowhere was safe.

Julian spared half a glance at the princess, knowing full well what her response would be to his next statement.

"I hope you like camping."

CHAPTER ELEVEN

Genevieve

"Camping?!"

"Yes, camping. As in, sleeping outdoors in a field, preferably a forest, with absolutely nobody around and –"

"Julian, I know what camping is. I just haven't experienced it before, given that I was *locked in a tower for twelve years* and –"

"And you're a princess," Julian finished for her. "Yes. I know."

Evie frowned for nobody to see. Something was wrong with Julian. *Well, something has been wrong for a while now, but this is different. Something happened to him when I was in the tailor's shop.*

She hurried along behind him, struggling to keep up with Julian's long legs even as his grip tightened on her arm. The town was well behind them now; Evie had to wonder what he was so concerned about. Back at the marketplace she'd thought Julian was worried about the young men who kept stealing glances at her. It had reassured Evie to know that he was looking out for her, but it became quickly apparent this extended to more than keeping away amorous youths.

"Julian, please, slow down!" Evie insisted when they reached a tall, ancient oak tree. It signalled the beginning of a forest so large that she couldn't see where it ended.

He turned, letting go of Evie's arm in the process. Though his eyes were on hers it seemed altogether like Julian was looking through her, instead. She didn't like it. It was only when he took the basket of food Evie had been precariously holding against her chest that he finally seemed to see her.

"Your dress is nice," Julian mumbled before looking away.

The comment should have made Evie happy – had he complimented on the dark green, leaf-embroidered fabric outside the tailor's shop then she'd have been ecstatic. As it were, Evie knew Julian was deflecting from telling her what was really going on. But the two of them

107

had been doing that to each other from the very beginning, so she sighed and moved past Julian into the forest. He wordlessly followed.

"Was it expensive?" he asked after ten minutes. Evie almost laughed, then slid her hand into one of the pockets sewn into the dress and threw a number of coins at Julian without looking to see if he caught them. Going by the string of curses he bit out she could only assume each and every one of them fell to the forest floor.

"Not so expensive as to be worried," she said, slowing her steps until Julian had finished picking up the coins. "The woman working in the shop loved my hair so much that she gave me a discount, I think. Is my hair meant to charm people, Julian? What did you weave into it?"

He glanced at her. "It shouldn't charm people, *per se.* But it's meant to disarm them, and make them trust you."

"Why would you put that in my *hair?*"

"So that nobody bothers us with suspicious questions," Julian answered simply. "The fact you got a well-fitting dress out of it is an unexpected benefit."

This time Evie *did* blush at the mention of her new clothes. It was an adult dress, made for a woman instead of a child. It cinched in at her waist and accentuated her curves without squeezing or hurting her, and the wide

108

skirt actually fell below her knees. It was cut low across her shoulders, exposing Evie's collarbones and the hollow of her throat. It was still a far cry from the opulent dresses she remembered being popular in Willow back when she was a child, but it was a fine improvement upon what she'd been wearing before.

Evie spun on the spot before jumping onto a fallen tree trunk. She grinned at Julian. "It really is a nice dress. I forgot what proper clothes felt like."

Julian was silent. Even an hour or two ago he'd have likely passed comment about how it wouldn't surprise him if Evie had *never* known what being in proper clothes was like, simply to insult her. But now he had nothing to say.

Something is wrong, Evie thought, more sure than ever before. *If I ask him what's happened will he simply ignore me again?*

And so the two of them weaved through the forest in silence for a while, Evie leading the way even though she didn't know where she was going. Her hair continued to unravel as it had been doing since that morning until it was once more long enough to trip her up; by the time the braid became completely undone the sun had set over the trees, casting the pair of them in pre-emptive twilight.

"Julian, are we going in the – ouch!"

"Will you watch what you're doing, you idiot?!" Julian exclaimed, dropping the basket of food in order to catch Evie before she fell to the forest floor. Her hair was entangled around a low-hanging branch, preventing Evie from walking any further until she was set free.

She stared at him dolefully. "I wasn't the one who wanted to leave the road so urgently. Why haven't you magicked my hair back into a braid, anyway?"

Evie thought Julian wasn't going to reply as he delicately unwound her hair from the branch. It always unnerved her to see him use his hands for such small, everyday tasks when she knew how much power he could hold in them.

But there was no magic sizzling in them now. There was no magic around Julian at all.

"I can't enchant your hair right now," he admitted. "Not until we find another town where someone else's magic can cover the trail of me doing it."

Evie flinched when her hair snagged on a thorn-covered vine twisting along the branch. Julian pulled out a knife from somewhere within his voluminous cloak and cut the offending greenery to pieces before gently removing it from her hair.

"I didn't know magic left a trail," Evie said, voice quiet as if she were whispering a secret.

Julian nodded sagely, though he didn't look at her.

"All magic does. An experienced tracker can find a specific wizard or magician if they know what to look for."

"And...someone is looking for you? Or...me?"

Eventually, with one final twist of his fingers, Julian set Evie's hair free. He indicated for her to sit down on one of the tree's massive, twisting roots, then knelt down behind her, pulled out a comb from his bag and got to work untangling her hair from the bottom-up.

"Julian, you really don't have to do that," Evie began, feeling her face grow hot even as the air slowly grew cooler around them. When night fell she imagined it would be cold this far inside the forest.

He chuckled humourlessly. "If I don't want you to become a permanent fixture of the forest I'll have to. Do you really want to entangle yourself on every branch, thorn and flower in this place?"

"No..."

"I could still cut it, you know."

Evie gasped at the thought, outraged. "You know I won't allow that!"

"Then tell me why."

The request was so softly made Evie thought she had imagined it at first. Julian had asked her about her hair before, of course, but she'd resolutely kept silent on the matter. Part of her still wanted to keep her answer to herself, though not for her original reason. Yes, Evie's memories of life in the palace were all the proof she had of who she was. For a girl with no material possessions who'd lived a solitary existence, they were more important than diamonds.

But Evie no longer lived in a lonely nightmare in the tower, and over the past three weeks she'd had more of a life travelling with Julian than she'd ever had before, even when she lived in the palace. Though she'd always treasure her childhood memories, they were no longer quite as precious as they once were.

"In the evening," Evie began; her voice took on an almost sing-song quality to it. She recognised the shift in tone as belonging to her mother, and she smiled. "In the evening before I went to bed, whenever my mother was home in the palace, she would come to my chambers with a comb as golden as my father's hair, and a brush so soft it would put a baby's hair to shame. Well, that's what mama said, anyway."

"Whenever she was home?" Julian interjected politely. Evie could hear him working through knots and tangles in the lower half of her hair; she shivered pleasantly to think of how it would feel when he reached her scalp.

She tilted her head backwards to look at him. "She wasn't home often. She was always travelling with my uncle."

There was something about the way Julian's eyes shone that made Evie think he was about to set the forest alight. But then she blinked and the glow disappeared, suggesting that all she'd seen was some last ray of sun flashing within his blue irises.

When Julian put his hands on either side of Evie's head to tilt it back to its original position she didn't protest. His fingers brushed against her neck. She resisted the urge to move closer to them – to feel them dig into her skin instead of merely whispering across it.

"So your mother would comb your hair, and you treasure the memory, and that's why you don't wish to cut it?" Julian asked, so matter-of-factly that Evie scowled, all previous unruly thoughts about the man vanished from her mind.

"Well when you put it like that it sounds stupid," she complained. "But I was eight, and I never got to see her much, and she would be so gentle and sing songs to me and tell me how beautiful my hair was."

"When you put it like that it *still* sounds stupid," Julian remarked, sliding the comb through the roots of Evie's hair until it no longer snagged even once. He worked his fingers through it, separating her hair into three sections before beginning to braid it. "Though I understand, I guess."

Evie hesitated before asking a question that had been on her mind for days. She twisted her hands in her lap, wondering if Julian would avoid answering her as he had with everything else so far.

"What is it you wish to ask me?" he murmured, so close to Evie's ear that she let out a cry of surprise. He snickered. "If it's about my childhood I'll do my best to answer you, since you've told me about your hair."

Fighting against the throbbing of her heart, Evie asked, "Where are your parents? Were you close with them?"

"Both dead." A pause. "I was closer with my mother than I was my father, but then she died when I was fifteen. Her death brought me and my father closer together than we had been before."

"When did your father die?"

"About twelve years ago," Julian replied. His fingertips grew a little rougher against Evie's scalp as he answered her, but then they slackened once more when he reached her neck.

"How old were you?"

"Eighteen."

"Ahh."

Evie could feel Julian frowning even though she couldn't see him. "What is 'ahh' supposed to mean?" he asked, making quick work of the rest of her hair as he braided it down her back.

"I've been wondering about your age for a while now, since you act like such an old man."

He clucked his tongue. "I'm ten years older than you, you brat."

"Not old enough to act like my father."

"When have I ever acted like your father?!"

Evie turned her head; Julian had finished braiding her hair and was beginning to coil it around his hand like a rope. She couldn't help but laugh, seeing him kneeling amongst pine needles and leaves and dirt with an affronted expression upon his face.

"You scold me all the time," she said, "and tell me what to do. And warn me not to misbehave, and –"

"That's because you'd die half a dozen times every day if I didn't," he complained, finishing winding up Evie's hair before flinging it over her shoulder and watching the braid fall into her lap. "I wouldn't say that's me acting like your father. I think you've just spent far too long away from people that you've forgotten what it's like to be looked after."

"Sometimes I think the same thing about you," Evie mumbled, looking away from Julian as she stood up. Her braid was still long enough to trail on the ground, but she

115

could easily hold it up from the forest floor in her hand. "Thank you for fixing my hair."

"It's just as much for my benefit as it is for yours," he said, ignoring Evie's first comment. He stood up, brushing leaves from his cloak before making his way further into the forest. Evie picked up the long-forgotten basket of food from the ground, replacing a few apples that had rolled out of it.

He said that the first time he fixed my hair, Evie thought as she wordlessly followed Julian beneath the murky boughs of the trees. *Yet if he truly only wanted to keep it out of the way he would never have spent so much time and magic on it.*

The two wound their way deeper and deeper into the forest until Evie was stumbling over unseen roots rather than her hair. She was cold, and tired, and her feet hurt, and her eyes could scarcely make out anything in front of her. But just as she was about to complain Julian stopped in front of her.

"We'll camp here for the night," he said. "I can hear a stream close by. Can you go and fill up our water skins?"

Numbly Evie did as she was told. All she could think about was warming up by a fire and falling asleep. But when she returned from the stream it didn't seem as if Julian was preparing a fire at all.

116

"We can't risk the smoke," was all he said, answering the question on Evie's face without telling her anything about who he didn't want to see said smoke. She grimaced.

Tonight was going to be a long, cold night.

CHAPTER TWELVE

Julian

Evie was shivering in the tent and there was nothing Julian could do.

The tent was made of hide, and it kept the wind and water out, but that didn't stop it from being cold. Even with the two of them taking up most of the space within it the air still had a bite to it.

It's never summer in the middle of a forest at midnight, Julian thought, glancing at the huddled figure turned away from him on his right. Evie had taken the top layer of her dress off – insisting she didn't want to wrinkle it – but that left her in a white underdress that was too thin to provide much warmth. The blanket Julian had given her wasn't much thicker, either; given that he usually used magic to heat up he'd never thought much about carrying a heavier one.

"Are you sure you can't light a fire?" Evie asked after a while, the words coming out a little unevenly as her teeth chattered. Julian felt wretched about the fact he couldn't, since he was warm simply by virtue of having honed fire magic within himself for so long. He was unlikely to feel cold for the rest of his life.

"You know I can't," he replied, not unkindly. He watched as Evie shifted her long braid of hair over her shoulder, hugging it closely to her chest as if it might provide some warmth. Julian reached a hand out to comfort her, then thought better of it and pulled it back. "Were you ever this cold in the tower?"

In the darkness Evie nodded. "There were times in winter I thought I'd die. I was never sent enough firewood to sufficiently warm up the room, and I had to forgo heating my bathwater for much of the season. Not the most pleasant of memories."

"I hadn't thought about the fact you must have been sent supplies," Julian admitted. He inched over a little closer to Evie, deciding that if she was too cold to sleep then the least he could do was talk to her until she was exhausted enough to fall into unconsciousness. He could have knocked her out with barely a hint of magic, but if the people tracking them down knew what they were looking for then they'd work out Julian's location immediately.

"Twice a day for twelve years," Evie said. She looked over her shoulder at Julian, eyes shining in the darkness. "You'd have thought whoever banished me could have at least ensured I had enough to eat and didn't freeze in winter."

Especially since it was your father, or uncle as the case may be, Julian mused. But Francis had said the king loved Genevieve; was his love so easily broken that he would doom his false daughter to spend more than half her life starving?

"Why is it so *cold?!*" Evie exclaimed a moment later in frustration. She huddled into herself as tightly as she could. "It's almost July. *July.* It should not be so cold."

"The depths of evergreen forests are their own little worlds," Julian said, staring up at the hide tent above them as if he could see straight through it. "In some countries there are entire races who rule the forests, and the lakes, and all the hidden places humans should never dwell upon for very long. Magical people who can look like exactly like you but are as dissimilar from humans as can be."

When he heard Evie shift over to face him Julian resisted smiling. He had hooked her with a tale enticing enough for her to forget the cold; he just had to keep it

120

that way.

"Have you met them before?" she asked. "These people?"

Julian nodded. "Once or twice. Both encounters were pleasant affairs, truth be told. They were amused by my powers. I think, had I not been a wizard, I would not have made it out of their forest alive."

Evie sidled a little closer to Julian, her eyes rapt and alert. This time he *did* smile, for how could he not? She wanted to hear more about the world – to counter her ignorance with knowledge. It was a feeling Julian could more than relate to.

"You said they live in lakes, too. Are they fish?"

He chuckled, then raised his hands above him. There was just enough difference in the levels of dark shadows inside the tent that Julian could make vague, fuzzy silhouettes appear upon its faded surface. He twisted his hands into a horse's head, then a seal, and then a fox.

"They take on many shapes," he explained. "Water horses and sleek-skinned seals by the shore, or murky-faced merpeople deep below the surface. The one I met was a fox, though. I don't think he wished to be one."

"I would rather be a fox and have the freedom to roam about than be trapped as a human in a tower," Evie said, reaching her own hands out to attempt to recreate

121

the fox Julian had made. Hers was smaller than his, and for a few moments they amused themselves by dancing the make-believe animals across the tent. Then Evie brought her hands back to her chest and shivered. "Are there really magical people like that, Julian, or did you just make them up to distract me?"

He raised an eyebrow at the ludicrous suggestion. "Do I strike you as the kind of person who could make such creatures up?"

"I'm not sure," Evie admitted. "I don't know much about you, truth be told."

"You know enough."

"Then that must mean there's not all that much to you."

"You wound me, Princess Genevieve."

An awkward pause followed Julian's words. Evie stared at him with wide eyes. "You haven't called me that with any sincerity even once before now. What changed?"

Julian looked away. "Nothing. Everything. I don't know. I guess I believe your story now, whereas I doubted it before."

"And why is that?"

He didn't want to tell her about what the king had done, or that her real father was his brother, or that it had been Julian's father who had spirited Evie away to her prison in Thorne tower. He didn't want to tell her about the fact Francis wished for Evie to stay as far away from Willow as possible, or that the king was looking for her.

He wanted Evie to stay just the way she was, unspoiled by the cruelty of her selfish family.

"Come here, Evie."

She hesitated. "What do you mean?"

"I mean come here," Julian repeated, indicating for her to lie closer to him. With one fluid motion he pulled his shirt away from his body, much to Evie's surprise. He grimaced at the look on her face. "I'm much warmer than you. It's the magic in me. Consider this my attempt at rectifying the fire problem."

Evie reached out a hesitant hand to touch Julian's chest but, upon feeling just how warm his skin was, forgot all her doubts and cuddled in as close as she possibly could. Julian resisted the urge to flinch away from her chilly, clammy touch.

"Why did you not tell me to do this earlier?" she demanded, voice muffled against Julian's shoulder as she eagerly wrapped her arms around him. "I'd have fallen asleep hours ago!"

"Yes, and I'd still be awake," Julian mused.

Evie looked up at him through her golden eyelashes. "What do you mean?"

"I mean that you're annoying. I thought you knew that by now."

"If I were the warm one and you were cold I'd have offered to do this from the very beginning."

Julian sighed good-naturedly. "I know. That doesn't change anything, though. Now settle down and go to sleep."

"I know you're only offering to do this to deflect from answering my questions, you know," Evie said after a while. Her body temperature had risen enough that Julian no longer wished to recoil from her, and found to his horror that he was enjoying the feeling of having her lying there against him.

"Go to sleep," he repeated, the words becoming muffled in Evie's hair. Her long braid snaked across the floor of the tent behind her; Julian wondered how she even coped with such a frustrating abundance of hair when sleeping.

If she had a husband he would insist she cut it, just so that it didn't interfere when they –

"Julian?"

He shook his head to remove any and all traces of such a dangerous train of thought. "What is it?" he

124

asked, a little sharper than he intended.

Evie's breath tickled against Julian's skin, setting his nerves on edge. When she shifted position one of her thighs ended up far too close to his groin; he closed his eyes and willed unconsciousness to take over as quickly as humanly possible.

"Have you been with many women before?" Evie asked, a question no other adult could likely ask in such an innocent manner. "Whilst you were travelling, I mean. Or before that, when you were younger."

Julian sighed. "Why are you asking me that?"

"Because I was –"

"Locked in a tower. Forget I asked."

He didn't answer her question, hoping that Evie would eventually move on from it and fall asleep. Her fingers just barely pressed into his back, sending a shiver running up his spine. Julian tried to ignore it, but then Evie dug her nails in a little more insistently.

He grabbed onto her hair without thinking and pulled Evie's face up to look at him. "What are you doing?" he growled. "Go to sleep!"

But her eyes were determined. "Why won't you answer my question?"

"Just what is that you want from me, Evie?"

"Stories," she said. "Experience. Why can't I get to know what *living* feels like, after so long on my own?"

God damn it, Julian thought, irritated beyond belief at Evie's infallible logic. For hadn't he only just acknowledged and approved of her thirst to learn of the world around her?

He hung his head in resignation; overgrown locks of his hair brushed against Evie's face. "I've been with a few women. There. Happy now?"

"No."

"And why not?"

"You didn't explain *anything*," she protested. "What were the women like? Was it fun? What did they think of you?"

"I suppose you could just touch me and find out!"

Julian had meant to be mocking; Evie *was* touching him already, after all. But when she glanced up at him the expression on her face suggested she'd taken him seriously.

"I can?" she whispered. Her voice hitched on the question in a way that drove Julian wild. Was she really *that* excited by the prospect? It was flattering, to say the least.

But dangerous. Too dangerous. Evie was a princess, and Julian was protecting her. It would be a huge violation of her trust, not to mention how inappropriate it was and –

"Fine," he muttered, immediately regretting the word the second he saw Evie grin in delight. "You have five minutes to bother me; after that you're going to sleep without another word. Got it?"

"Got it," she said, nodding seriously, though there was a mischievous glint in her eyes that suggested Evie might just push past the five minutes anyway.

But then her fingertips ran down his back, and Julian forgot to care. He hadn't been with a woman in a while, given that he'd largely kept to himself the past couple of years, and his nerves had been shot ever since he'd kept Evie company after her nightmare.

This is wrong, he thought. *This is a mistake.*

Evie slid her hands across Julian's waist until she reached his stomach before creeping up to his chest. Her eyes followed her fingertips, watching the way they pressed into his skin almost reverently.

"...having fun?" Julian muttered after a couple of minutes had passed. Evie nodded, though she bit her lip instead of saying anything. She wasn't looking at him, instead casting her eyes downward to the laces of his trousers.

Lord help me.

When Evie's hands roamed towards his waist Julian jerked away.

"Please don't," he said, pulling Evie's hands back up until they were cupped between his own, in front of his face. "I can assure you that you don't want to do that."

Evie merely frowned in annoyance. "How can you possibly know what I want to do, Julian? And I still have two minutes. Why can't I –"

He planted a kiss against her hand, the action silencing her mid-sentence. She stared into his eyes, which he knew were likely too bright with the promise of barely-fettered magic. Evie slid the hand Julian had kissed away from his own, stroking the line of his jaw with about as much force as a feather. When she reached his hair Evie pushed it back, running her hand through it until it fell across his face, where it had lain before.

She was pressed right up against him; every curve of her body finding another inch of Julian's skin to touch. He couldn't take it; it was unbearable.

"Why can't I want this?" Evie asked, managing to get her question out in its entirety this time. "Am I really so annoying, Julian?"

He held his breath for a second. Two. Three.

"Yes," Julian said, and then his mouth was on hers. He rolled Evie onto her back, hands roving beneath her dress to cling to her hips, her waist, her breasts –

anything he could find. Evie eagerly reciprocated, flinging her arms around Julian's neck even as her legs did the same around his waist.

He groaned when she bucked against his groin. She parted her lips to let in his tongue; Julian imagined doing something similar with an altogether harder body part. He pressed down upon her, burying Evie into the blanket, the floor of the tent, the soft ground of the forest below, until there was nowhere deeper he could push her.

He needed more. He needed –

"We need to stop," Julian gasped, wrenching himself away from Evie as if she were made of flames. He held a hand over his eyes. "Good lord, Evie, we can't do this. I can't do this."

There was nothing but the sound of laboured breathing for a while. Eventually Evie asked, very quietly, "Is it because you don't like me, or because I'm Princess Genevieve?"

"The latter," he replied. "Of course it's the latter. I'd never have gone this far if I didn't like you."

"...thank you for your honesty," was all Evie said, and then she turned from him.

Julian didn't dare open his eyes again that night.

CHAPTER THIRTEEN

Genevieve

Neither Julian nor Evie brought up their first night sharing a tent together for the remaining part of their journey to Willow, though they spent another week and a half sleeping inside it every night. But whenever they camped deep into the chilly depths of a forest Julian wordlessly removed his shirt and allowed Evie to huddle close to him, for which she was grateful.

But her heart hurt, and Evie could neither understand it nor do anything about it. Julian had thrown away her burgeoning feelings before she had even accepted them for what they were. She knew that, at the very least, she should be happy that Julian had not rejected her out of dislike but, rather, out of a sense of duty and responsibility. Given the fact he'd been looking out for her ever since he'd saved her from those men on the road, Evie could hardly be surprised by this turn of events.

That doesn't make his rejection sting any less, she thought sadly as she finally entered the city of Willow. Julian was walking a few paces ahead of her, keeping to himself. He was on high alert for – something. Or someone. Evie couldn't tell; it wasn't as if Julian had informed her about what was going on. But his antsy energy had her on edge, too, making it impossible for Evie to appreciate the beautiful, intricate architecture of the city in which she'd been born.

It was both alien and achingly familiar to her, as if Evie's mind itself had invented the place in a dream. Not that she'd dreamt of cities or palaces or even her royal heritage all that much over the past few days. No, all she'd dreamt about as she and Julian made their awkward way towards Willow was Julian himself.

Evie couldn't stop thinking about the way he'd looked at her before he gave in and kissed her, or the ferocity with which he'd pushed her below him. The weight of Julian on top of her – the feeling of having every inch of his skin against hers – had been driving her insane ever since. Evie had wanted more. *Needed* more.

But Julian had pulled away.

Damn him being responsible and righteous just when I craved for him not to be, she cursed, dolefully watching the man stalk through the throng of the crowd. All Evie had wanted over the past few days was to ignore Julian until he kissed her with desperate longing once more, but though she'd followed through on the former Julian had not done the same with the latter.

And now it's too late. We've reached Willow and soon I will probably never seen Julian again. I should not have ignored him simply because he hurt my pride.

But was it really her pride Julian had hurt? Evie hadn't spent enough time with other people to have any pride in herself as a woman. Then was it her pride as a princess that he'd broken? The fact that he'd rejected her for the one part of her that she could not change – a part of her she could have demanded he accept if she'd really wanted to?

Evie laughed bitterly. *I could never do that.*

Julian stopped to look back at her, concerned. "What's the matter?"

"Nothing," she said, waving him away. "Nothing at all. I'm just nervous." It wasn't untrue; Evie's stomach had been lurching and roiling all morning. She hadn't eaten anything at breakfast – much to Julian's surprise.

His face softened. "Everything will be fine, Evie. And

if it's not...well, that's what I'm here for. And on the subject of what I'm here for..."

Evie frowned as Julian regarded her critically. She *had* to frown, otherwise she'd blush as red as a summer apple beneath his gaze. "What is it?"

"I think it's probably safe to work some magic on your hair once more," Julian said, darting his head back and forth as he looked for somewhere quieter to perform the enchantment. "And you could do with a more expensive dress."

Evie picked at the sleeve of the one she was wearing. "But I like this one. It's like a forest."

"I never said you had to get rid of it, only that you need a new one. You want to look your best to meet your parents, do you not? And your brother?"

She froze at the mention of her brother, Louis. Evie had chosen not to think about him ever since Julian had first brought him up. This was partially due to him telling her that Louis was sickly and unlikely to survive childhood, but for the most part it was because Evie couldn't imagine having a sibling. He would be the age she was when she was sent to the tower, after all. It was unfathomable. Unknowable.

It scared Evie to no end.

"Evie?"

She shook her head. "Yes, okay. Let's make me look my best. Only..."

Now it was Evie's turn to cast a critical eye over Julian. The wizard was hidden beneath his stained and ragged cloak, and though most of his hair was tied back there remained a few errant strands covering his eyes. Julian's stubble had grown to the point of it almost being considered a beard; Evie longed to see it gone.

"No," Julian said, upon realising what Evie's expression meant. "No. I'm fine just the way I am."

Evie crossed her arms over her chest. "If *I* need to look more presentable when I'm already in a nice dress then you definitely need to look better, Julian."

He pointed at her. "You and I both know that it's your hair that's the problem. It's a travesty."

"Still not cutting it."

"Even if I agree to cut *mine*?"

Evie faltered. It was an appealing bribe. However...

"No. I don't want to cut my hair...even if it's only for another few days. And besides, you *have* to cut your hair."

Julian cocked an eyebrow. "Oh?"

"I'm the princess. You have to do what I say."

So much for never using that against him.

To her relief, Julian laughed. "If that is the only thing you can think of to demand of me then fine, I will. But let me fix your hair first, *then* we can set about getting new clothes and fixing me."

"You don't need *fixed*," Evie muttered as Julian pulled her down a near-abandoned alleyway. Had he not been a wizard Evie would never have gone down such a street; even now there were hungry eyes on them, busy calculating how much money they were likely to be carrying. But then Julian's eyes began to glow, and his fingertips turned Evie's hair to liquid gold, and they scurried away in fear.

Evie sighed contentedly as Julian enchanted her hair. She'd missed the feeling of it – of hot, bubbling magic coursing through every strand as he weaved and braided the lot of it into so elaborate a hairstyle even the aristocrats of Willow would be envious.

When Julian was done and pulled his fingertips away from her scalp Evie felt a keening sense of regret. It was, most probably, the last time he would ever work his magic on her.

Well, in the literal sense, she amended, watching longingly as Julian rolled out a kink in his shoulders and shook his hair from his eyes. When he smiled at her his expression was so guarded against her it hurt Evie's heart.

"Shall we go shopping, then?" he asked. But Evie shook her head, and Julian's formal smile disappeared.

"What's wrong?"

"I...think I want to buy a dress by myself. Can we find an inn first so that we can meet back there when we're both done?"

The meaning behind her words was plain for Julian to translate: *I can't pretend that everything is fine between us any longer.*

He regarded Evie for so long she almost repeated her request. But then, finally, Julian inclined his head, then pulled a small bag of coins from his cloak and proffered them to her. She took it wordlessly, being careful not to touch his hands. They were abuzz with magic, as if Julian could no longer contain it for some reason.

"Let's find a good inn for the night, then," he said, "though I doubt any inn will seem *good* once you return to the palace."

"Trust me," Evie replied, lips quirking into a smile despite her bad mood, "anything will feel like luxury after spending eleven days sleeping in a tent."

Julian snickered. "Fair point. Here's hoping neither of us need ever find ourselves in a tent again."

Evie didn't reply; she merely followed Julian out of the alleyway and down the main street as he searched for an inn. Going by the purposeful way he wound his way through the crowd he already had a place in mind. But it didn't matter how lovely the room was that Julian paid for Evie to sleep in that night – she knew she would be sleeping in it alone.

And though camping had been hell, and she had hated most every part of it, it was a hell Evie would gladly live through again and again if it meant she did not have to say good bye to Julian.

CHAPTER FOURTEEN

Julian

Julian watched his reflection in the mirror as if he did not recognise the person staring back at him. For the first time in months – years, even – he was clean-shaven. His dark hair was shorter than it had been in over a decade, though it still fell below his ears. The barber had slicked it back, though, keeping it out of Julian's eyes and leaving his face self-consciously visible.

Julian had purchased a dark, pine-green waistcoat shot through with gold thread that afternoon, to wear alongside a white shirt, beige trousers and ebony knee-high boots. An olive-coloured longcoat with gold buttons finished the entire ensemble. Looking at himself wearing such finely made clothes deeply unsettled Julian; he looked like his father in his heyday, though his blue eyes belonged to his mother.

She would be happy to see me finally dressed so appropriately, Julian mused as he took a swig from the tankard of ale he'd had ordered up to his room. It was his third since returning to the inn. Though he knew Evie had also returned by virtue of the magic in her hair Julian was yet to see or speak to her, namely because he dared not leave his room. He didn't know *what* to say. But the sun was low in the sky on what would likely be their final day together – an ever-present reminder that he was fast running out of time in which to be honest with her.

"I am a coward," Julian murmured, giving his outfit one final inspection before finishing his ale and leaving his room. He could sit inside it alone no longer, agonised by all his thoughts and actions over the past month. Either Julian would find solace in the tavern attached to the inn or by walking along the paved stone roads that followed the river which split Willow in two.

When he reached the tavern in question Julian was relieved to see that Evie wasn't there, though he already knew she was still in her room. But her very presence in the back of his mind kept Julian on edge at all times until he could scarcely bear to be conscious, so he decided going for a walk would perhaps give him enough distance to calm himself down.

139

"She's the princess," he said aloud, "she's the princess and she's nearly home. Your job is almost done." Julian made his way out into the lovely July evening, ignoring the looks of interest several young women threw his way. He'd forgotten what it was like to be admired like that, having spent so long hiding beneath his hair and beard and cloak.

Evie looked at me like that even when she couldn't see my face properly, Julian mused as he made his way towards the river. *But, then again, she'd spent most of her life locked up alone. Her standards are probably pretty low.*

He chuckled at the thought as he absorbed the last of the evening's warmth. If Evie had been with him her hair would be set alight by the sunset, garnering sighs of admiration and envy everywhere she went. It upset Julian to think he'd probably enchanted her hair for the final time that afternoon.

Don't think about that. Don't think about her. *Think about literally anything else.*

But how could Julian refrain from thinking about Evie when he was only in Willow because of her? When he was embroiled in the mess her family had created – the same mess that Julian's father had somehow been involved in before his death? Julian needed answers just as much as Evie herself did. He could only hope that bringing her back to the palace would not be the mistake

Francis Saule was convinced it was.

I'm here to protect her if things go awry, Julian reminded himself. *The moment something seems wrong I'll whisk Evie away never to be seen again.*

He entertained himself with the idea of taking Evie to see the forests where the fair folk lived. She'd been interested in their magical, shape-shifting ways, after all. Perhaps Julian might even be able to find the creature trapped as a fox once more to prove to Evie that it existed. He almost laughed at his previous assertion that his thirteen years of travelling had been unremarkable; had Julian really believed such a thing? For now all he could think of were the places Evie would love to see, both the wonders of the modern world and the relics of the past.

A few right turns – and several wrong ones – later and Julian made it to the river. The low angle of the sun had turned it to shining, flashing silver, so blinding he had to half-close his eyes simply to look at it. He leant on the intricate iron railing that separated the paved road from the river and heaved out a sigh.

Willow is a beautiful city, Julian supposed, though he reckoned it had become more beautiful simply by virtue of him having spent so many years away from it. If there was enough time in the morning, and if he worked up the nerve to ask her, Julian decided he'd take Evie for a walk through the expansive parks in the very centre of the city

141

before escorting her to the palace.

It would be a smart idea to do so, he realised. *The more people who see her in public looking so obviously like Princess Genevieve then the safer she'll be.* But the people of Willow hadn't seen their princess in twelve years; would they recognise her? Julian certainly hadn't believed Evie's story of her parentage at first, so why would complete strangers have reason to think she was their princess?

Because they aren't cynical like me, and she looks every part King Pierre's daughter. Even though she isn't. I suppose it's a good thing Francis looks so much like his brother.

"You really brought her here. You brought her to *Willow*."

Julian scowled at the sound of the man's voice. "Are you kidding me? Just where did you come from?"

Francis Saule wasn't amused. "You're distracted; you didn't even notice me approaching. Where is Genevieve?"

"Safe."

"But where?"

"Telling you that will compromise her safety, don't you think?"

The older man leant on the railing beside Julian,

casting his solemn gaze across the river. "You do not trust me."

"And why should I?" Julian laughed humourlessly. "You've followed, and spied on us, whilst only giving me information as you yourself deemed it pertinent. That doesn't provide me with many reasons to trust you."

"Yet you know enough not to trust my brother, or the people he's sent out to find you. So why are you in Willow?"

Julian hung his head. "Because Evie wants to go home. I'm not going to disregard her wishes."

He knew Francis was staring at him, disbelief plain on his face even though Julian wasn't looking at it. "Have you not told her *anything*, Julian? Is she still in the dark?"

"Of course she is!" he spat out, rounding on the man with barely-contained fury. Out of the corner of his eye he saw that they were gathering the attention of several curious bystanders, so Julian lowered his voice and forced himself to calm down. He glared at Francis. "Why should her worldview be destroyed after everything she's been through?"

The king's brother merely smiled sadly. "Because that's the only way to keep her safe. Why can't you just spirit her far from here, away from the drama of Willow and its king?"

"Because then I'd be no better than any of you, doing as you please without once thinking about what Evie herself wants."

"But you're not truly thinking of what she wants, either," Francis countered. "You haven't told her the truth about what's going on. How can Genevieve know what she wants when she's ignorant of so much?"

"She's been doing just fine until now," Julian snarled, before turning from the man and stalking away. If he stayed any longer in Francis' company then he'd probably use magic, and that would draw too much attention in such a public spot, and then Julian would be found. It was bad enough to have been seen viciously arguing with someone by the river in the first place.

At least I no longer fit the description of a scraggly, ragged-clothed wizard, Julian reasoned, trying desperately to look on the brighter side of things. *If anyone looking for me hears of my current appearance then they will not think that I am me.*

Julian made it back to the inn with a head full of stormy thoughts. It was so full, in fact, that he had forgotten to check where Evie currently was, and it was only upon entering the tavern that he realised she was at the bar, being served a cup of wine, surrounded by admirers.

She wasn't in as elaborate a dress as Julian would have expected, given that it was supposed to be for returning to the palace, though Julian numbly thought that perhaps Evie had bought more than one given how much money he'd handed over to her.

Regardless, Evie looked breathtaking. The dress was a powder blue colour reminiscent of the ill-fitting clothing Julian had first found her in. The sleeves sat off her shoulders, and were slashed with a cream fabric embroidered with hundreds of tiny flowers. The bodice was similarly embroidered, whilst the sweeping material of the skirt was about an inch or two longer than Evie's magically braided hair.

She was the epitome of the sky, with her golden hair the sun and her dress the endless blue of summer. *So what does that make her eyes?* Julian wondered. *Emeralds don't live in the sky. Perhaps they are the forest.*

It was in that moment Julian finally realised why he'd bought the clothes *he* was wearing. They were the colours of the trees that had marked his journey with Evie all the way to Willow – broad leaved and evergreen, pale-branched and dark.

Just what have I become? Julian thought, laughing softly at his own ineptitude as he watched Evie from a safe distance away; she had not yet realised he was there. *I need another drink. All I can think of is her.*

And if all he could think of was Evie...how was he supposed to let her go?

CHAPTER FIFTEEN

Genevieve

Genevieve had never embraced so much attention before – not since she was a child, at least, and even then her father had largely kept her within the palace, so her experience with people was limited. The attention of tavern-goers was certainly different to the aristocrats who used to politely amuse her when they came to visit her mother and father, though the inn Julian had chosen was markedly more high-class than the ones they'd stayed in before.

And though Evie had chosen to forgo the formal gown she'd procured for returning to the palace in place of the one she'd bought solely for herself, she stood out. *It's because of my hair,* she thought, though Evie wasn't unhappy about this. Imbued with magic or not it was a part of her, and there was no sense in Evie wondering whether the rest of her would ever look as good as the woven, golden crown Julian had braided around her head.

Evie hadn't realised he'd done such a thing until she looked in the mirror to admire his handiwork. The rest of her hair fell to her ankles in a multitude of interlaced braids of varying thicknesses, and it was beautiful, but the woven crown was something else entirely. It was heartbreakingly intricate; Evie couldn't imagine the amount of thought the wizard must have put into styling it in such a way. And Julian had deliberately kept a few wispy strands of Evie's hair loose around her face, softening the look just enough that it seemed as if she had been born with her hair sitting this way instead of it being the work of genius magic.

For the first time in twelve years, in her well-fitting blue gown, matching slippers and sun-coloured crown around her head, Evie genuinely felt like a princess.

It was more bittersweet that she could ever have imagined.

Well, that's nothing that some wine cannot fix, Evie decided as she began drinking her second cup of the stuff. It was light and sweet – much unlike the wine she'd accidentally drank on the first night of her journey to Willow – but heady enough that Evie could feel it burning inside of her already. She thought back to how she'd so quickly fallen asleep that first time, never truly getting to experience the effects the alcoholic drink.

But tonight was different. Tomorrow Evie would make her way to the palace, to her mother and father and brother, and her life would change completely. One way or another she'd never have the opportunity to drink in a tavern under the guise of anonymity again, even though the attention her hair was getting was a far cry from what Julian would consider to be 'anonymous'.

He would be so angry with this much attention, she thought, laughing a little in the process. *He'd walk away from everyone to sit in the corner in a huff, and ignore any questions and greetings thrown his way.*

It was only in thinking this that Evie remembered she hadn't actually *seen* Julian since she'd pushed him away that afternoon. She could only assume he was somewhere in the inn.

She was too prideful to go and find him.

"If he wants to see me then *he* can find me," Evie muttered, knowing deep in her heart that if Julian didn't seek her out at some point that night then she'd probably cry into her pillow instead of falling asleep in a few hours. She didn't want this to be the way they left things between them – awkward, painfully formal, and silent.

"What was that, my lovely?"

Evie smiled for the young man who had spoken. His name was John, and he had pushed through several of his friends to stand by her side. "Oh, nothing," she replied. She held up her cup. "I was just thinking that this wine is delicious."

"Then I must buy you another one!"

"I have only just started my second," she protested. Evie could feel her cheeks growing rosy and warm from the stuff and knew she had to be careful. *Julian would be furious if I let down my guard enough to allow these men to get me drunk. He would think I haven't learned anything at all.*

Another of the men elbowed John out of the way. "We've never seen you around here before. Are you visiting your fiancé perhaps?"

Evie shook her head. "Family. I've been away from the city for a long time."

The man grinned. "Then you definitely need more wine to celebrate your return! We can show you around; Willow changes year on year on year. You must scarcely recognise it."

"I – I'm not sure," Evie admitted, for it was never as if she'd known much of the city in the first place. She could recognise most every stone of the palace and its grounds, and a few of the grand buildings which many of the members of her father's court lived in, but that was it.

"You don't want to be wandering the city at night," John said, though the excited look on his face suggested he hadn't said as much out of actual concern for Evie. "It's better to stay here and let us all keep you company. Are you staying here? Upstairs?"

"You can't possibly be travelling alone."

"She must have a lover, for sure."

Evie held her hands up as if they could stop the barrage of remarks being thrown her way. "There's nobody like that," she said, though it pained her to say it out loud. "I must admit I don't have much experience in that department."

The second man stared at her as if he couldn't believe his luck. "A lady so lovely as yourself? Your lack of experience must be rectified! What is the point of living if you don't explore everything it has to offer?"

That had been Evie's reasoning the night she somehow managed to convince Julian to answer her inane, intrusive questions. The night he let her touch him and almost lost control entirely. But hearing a stranger use such reasoning to try and charm Evie into his bed made her squirm uncomfortably. He wasn't thinking of her wellbeing, only his own pleasure at her hands.

Is this what Julian thought in the tent? Evie wondered miserably. *Did I put him in an awful, unwinnable position simply for my own amusement? But I didn't want to hold him to make him uncomfortable. I didn't want to do it to satisfy my curiosity for a night. I wanted...*

"And who might you be to 'rectify' the lady's lack of experience?" an achingly familiar voice demurred. "Something tells me I'm much more qualified to help her out than you, sir."

An arm snaked its way around Evie's waist, pulling her close before she had the chance to look up at the man she'd only just been thinking about. When she finally *did* look she froze.

The Julian beside her was not the Julian she knew.

His face was clean-shaven, revealing cheekbones Evie's mother might have said were chiselled by the gods had Julian appeared in one of her Greek mythology tomes. His black hair was slicked back to tuck around his ears, and there was a charming smile upon his lips that Evie had never seen him use before.

Julian's clothes were gorgeous and intricately designed, right down to the embossed patterns on the gold buttons of his longcoat. Evie had once asked him why he never dressed like the amber-eyed stranger who they'd seen weeks ago. Now she knew why.

Julian was beautiful, and he was gathering attention.

How he must hate that, Evie thought, when her brain finally kicked back into action. Julian tightened his grip on her waist and grinned at her, a twinkle in his blue eyes which for the life of her Evie could not work out if it was genuine or caused by magic. It might have been both. She almost thought her heart would stop. *If he keeps acting like this I might get the wrong idea.*

"Are these gentlemen bothering you, my lady?" Julian asked, much to the chagrin of the men in question.

"I'd say that you're the one bothering her!" John said, though Evie could tell by the look on his face that he knew he could not compete against Julian.

I wonder if I can compete against the women who like him, Evie thought, glancing around to see many lovely, excited faces watching him. When she caught the eye of one such lady she scowled at Evie; Evie in turn had to admit that it felt good to be envied for such a thing as claiming Julian's attention.

"Are you drunk?" she murmured up to him, so quietly nobody else heard.

His hand slid further down Evie's waist – a deliberate move that was noted by every one of Evie's admirers. "A little," he admitted. "Is that a problem?"

"Not that I can see. Are you here to rescue me?"

"If that is what you wish."

Evie's heart was pounding so loudly in her chest she wouldn't have been surprised if Julian could hear it. She inclined her head politely to the men who were staring at the pair of them, agog. "Thank you for your company, kind sirs," Evie said, "but it appears I must be whisked away. I hope you enjoy the rest of your evening."

Julian's hand nudged her away from the bar, though Evie was sure to grab her cup of wine before stepping away. They barely made it to a table at the back of the tavern before she heard the men muttering about how unlucky they'd been for Julian to have shown up.

"Luck had nothing to do with it," he said, smiling in an entirely satisfactory way as he stole the cup of wine from Evie's hand and drank the lot of it.

"Hey, that was mine!" she protested. He merely pushed her onto a softly padded bench that was built below a stained glass window before sliding in beside her. When he waved over at the bar the man behind it promptly brought over a flagon and another cup.

"And now we both have more," Julian replied, handing the man several coins before pouring Evie a new drink. "That's the beauty of having money."

Evie eyed him warily as she drank her wine. "Nobody would have been so quick to serve you had you looked the way you usually look."

"And yet that's still the beauty of money, for look how beautiful my money has made me."

She couldn't help but snort in disgusted amusement

at the comment, narrowly avoiding spilling wine over her new dress. "I never knew you were so narcissistic, Julian."

"Only when I have the outfit to support it, and the alcohol in my blood to keep it up."

Evie quirked her lips into half a smile, then looked away. "What did you mean that luck had nothing to do with you showing up when you did?"

"I may or may not have been in the tavern for an hour already, watching to see what would happen."

"And what did you think would happen?" Evie asked, close to outrage. Had Julian assumed she'd end up falling into bed with a stranger?

"Nothing, I suppose." He watched Evie out of the corner of his eye; she blushed. "Though I do recall a certain someone telling me they wanted to experience more of the world, including particularly...private affairs."

If Evie thought she'd been blushing before it was nothing compared to how hot her cheeks were now. "I didn't – that wasn't – I only wanted to experience such things with *you*, Julian!"

He put down his cup just as Evie did the same. She could scarcely look at him, horrified by her admission. But then Julian bent his head low until his lips were right by her ear; his breath tickled her skin.

"I guess that means I truly *am* the only one qualified

enough to help you out," he said, voice low and seductive in a way Evie had never heard before.

Her breathing hitched. "You're drunk, Julian. You're only saying this because you're drunk. You –"

He held a finger to Evie's lips to quieten her, then gently turned her face until her eyes were locked on his. They were dark in the dim light of the tavern – hardly blue at all – but around the rims of Julian's irises was the glow of ever-present magic Evie yearned to feel touch her.

Julian tucked a hand behind Evie's neck, edging her face so close to his own that she was sure he was going to kiss her. "Do you want to come up to my room?" he asked.

Evie nodded before he'd even finished the sentence, then Julian snapped his fingers and they were gone.

CHAPTER SIXTEEN

Julian

"You didn't – I thought you had to be careful with your magic right now?" Evie exclaimed when the two of them materialised inside Julian's room. "We could have used the stairs."

He laughed at the notion, cupping Evie's face between his hands before saying, "I don't think I could have waited that long." And then he kissed her, and kissed her, and kissed her, until Evie's lips grew swollen beneath his own and she let out an almost imperceptible moan in response.

Julian pushed her back towards the bed; when they

reached it Evie curled her hands into his shirt and broke away from his bruising kiss. Her cheeks were so attractively flushed Julian reached to kiss her again almost immediately.

When did she get so beautiful? he thought, through a haze of desire rapidly going unchecked. *She had always been a skinny, annoying brat. She –*

"Julian, slow down!" Evie bit out, breathing heavily as she once more pulled away from his lips. His hands were making quick work of the ribbons which laced up her bodice, hungry to feel the warmth of her skin beneath it.

He shook his head. "I can't. I don't want to."

"Those are two different things."

"Yes, and they both apply. Is there something wrong with that?"

It was Evie's turn to shake her head. She rubbed her fingers against the fabric of Julian's shirt, watching her hands as she did so. "No, there isn't. But what...what changed, Julian? Is it really the alcohol making you do all this?"

"Oh lord no," he said. He grazed his lips along Evie's jawline to her ear. "Nothing's changed. Not really. Unless you count the fact you turned my world upside down the moment I found you in the tower, in which case everything has changed."

Evie turned her head until her mouth found Julian's once more. "You said you couldn't do this. You said –"

"I know what I said. And it's...still true." He kissed her softly. "It's still true, but for one night all I want to do is ignore what I *should* do. I want to forget the responsibility I have towards getting you to the palace, unspoiled and in one piece."

To his surprise, Evie laughed. She reached up on her tiptoes to snake her arms around Julian's neck. "You've been *spoiling* me from day one, Julian. You and I both know you should have magicked me to Willow immediately and been done with me."

"You know precisely what I mean."

"Yes, but can I not make my own decisions on who I share my bed with...at least until I return to my parents?"

When Julian eased Evie's arms away from him and took a step back there was a fear in her eyes that he revelled in. It told Julian that she really wanted him. That the desire building up in Evie these past few weeks was very much as genuine as the desire Julian, in turn, felt for her.

He dropped to his knees in front of her, clasping her hands within his own. She looked down at him uncertainly even as he smiled at her.

"Spend your final night as 'Evie' with me, Princess Genevieve. Spend the night with me, so when the sun rises neither of us can regret a thing."

How the pair of them removed each other's clothes so quickly Julian could not fathom, but before he knew it all that was left to strip away were Evie's underdress and his shirt.

"Your new dress is beautiful, by the way," he said between kisses. The blue fabric was pooled on the floor around them, so Julian picked Evie up and deftly carried her over to the bed without stepping on it. She clung to him as he did so, trailing kisses along Julian's collarbone that left his skin blazing.

"Thank you," Evie replied, a genuine smile at the compliment lighting up her face. "It's my favourite colour. Your new clothes aren't too bad, either. I never knew you had such good taste."

He dropped Evie onto the bed and eagerly climbed on top of her. "There's a lot you don't know about me," he murmured, kissing the hollow of her throat as he did so. Julian was satisfied to feel her squirm at his touch.

She glanced down at him through heavy, golden eyelashes. "I thought you said there wasn't much to know about you?"

"*You* were the one who said that. I told you that you knew enough."

"So you were lying?"

When Julian felt one of Evie's legs slide against his own he grabbed hold of her knee and hitched it around his waist. Her eyes went wide as she felt a hardness against her navel that the loose folds of Julian's shirt had been concealing from her.

He smirked. "You knew enough for back then. Now you could do with learning some more."

Julian pulled his shirt up and over his head before making quick work of the buttons of Evie's underdress. He flung both garments to the floor. Though the young woman below him had spent much of their time together in various indecently ill-fitting clothes, Julian had somehow managed to avoid seeing Evie completely naked before now. For some reason he had imagined she would be small and skinny as she had been when he'd first saved her life, despite their night in the tent together and all other growing signs to the contrary.

But a month of eating as if Evie was afraid she'd be locked up once more with no food had done wonders for her body. Julian marvelled at the sight of her lying beneath him, face flushed with embarrassment as he continued to stare without uttering a word.

"I know, I'm still a brat," Evie muttered, but when she turned her face away from Julian he reached down, grabbed her chin to keep her in place and kissed her, hard.

"Clearly eating like a piglet for slaughter has been to

161

your benefit...and mine," Julian murmured. He bit her lower lip. His hands crawled over her chest. He watched as Evie's breathing accelerated with every slide of his fingertips across her skin; every gentle pinch of her flesh; every inch of friction between their two bodies.

Eventually she couldn't take it any longer. "Julian," she moaned. "This is torture."

"No; torture is listening to you talk all day with no escape or end in sight."

His mouth covered hers to swallow any retort she might have had, though Evie didn't seem to mind all that much. Julian's hands wound their way through her hair, though he had avoided touching it so far; the enchanted braids unravelled instantly, allowing him to properly slide his fingers against Evie's scalp. Though Julian knew the full length of her hair would get in the way of what the two of them were about to do next, he didn't care.

I can fix it in the morning, he thought, as Evie pushed her own fingers through Julian's hair in order to keep him as close to her lips as possible. *In the morning I'll be Julian Thorne, the wizard, and Evie will be Princess Genevieve. But not now.*

The next time Evie opened her mouth to beg Julian to stop teasing him he happily obliged. He was at his limit too, after all, and the desperate tug of his groin ached with every second he didn't do what his body demanded he do.

162

Evie cried in shock, though Julian held her close and resisted moving as much as possible until her kisses became hungry and insatiable once more. It wasn't long before her nails dug into his back, insisting that he go faster, and harder, and deeper, until Evie was a mess of gasps and tears and vicious pleasure beneath him.

I can't let her go, Julian thought, the realisation slashing through his blind lust like a knife in the dark. *I don't know what's waiting for her in the palace. I don't want to find out. Tomorrow I'll –*

But then it was Julian's turn to moan, for Evie shifted her hips and in the process undid him completely. He loomed above her on shaking arms, simultaneously exhausted and exhilarated. Every inch of his skin was shining wtth sweat; with glazed eyes he saw that Evie's was, too.

Julian gulped down a much-needed mouthful of air. "Are you –"

"Fine," Evie panted, a small smile curling her lips when Julian flung himself down beside her with a thump. "I'm fine. Better than fine."

"Good."

"Would you like some water?"

He glanced at her. Evie's hair was plastered to her forehead; her cheeks were so red they looked feverish. "I should be asking *you* that, not the other way around."

"I'm capable of looking after you when you need someone to, you know," Evie huffed, though her annoyance was short-lived when Julian pulled her into the crook of his arm and began smoothing her hair back.

"It's a good thing I'm not the one who needs looking after, then."

Evie kissed his shoulder before looking up at him. Her eyes glittered in the darkness. "Are you sure about that?"

"Fairly sure. You should get some sleep, Evie. Tomorrow will be a long, long day."

"I thought we weren't thinking about tomorrow?" she asked, frowning in concern. Julian squeezed her tighter against his side.

"You're right. We won't. But sleeping in an actual bed instead of a tent sounds great, does it not?"

Based on the look on Evie's contented face she readily agreed. By the time Julian's breathing returned to a normal, even pace she was already halfway to unconsciousness. *How can I not think about tomorrow?* he thought as he stared down at her. *No matter what happens, tomorrow will change everything.*

But before he could agonise over whether he'd be lying in bed alone once more the following evening, or whether he'd miraculously still have Evie curled up beside him, the overwhelming urge to sleep took over

Julian and he forgot all about his problems.

CHAPTER SEVENTEEN

Genevieve

When Genevieve awoke the sun was shining in her face and Julian was nowhere to be seen. She sat up stock straight, immediately alert, only for the man himself to enter through the door carrying a tray of food.

"Morning," Julian said, smiling slightly when he saw that Evie was no longer sleeping. She blushed and pulled up the bedsheets to cover her chest when she realised she was completely exposed. Julian merely laughed. "I saw a lot more of you last night. There's no need to be embarrassed."

Evie took the cup of water he handed her with a nod

of thanks. "Everything is different in the light of day," she said, glancing out of the window to the morning bustle of Willow down below.

Julian stiffened. "Are you saying you regret what happened?"

"No!" she exclaimed, quick to correct him. "No. Absolutely not. But, you know, in daylight people look different, and alcohol changes things, and –"

Evie's ramblings were cut off when Julian collapsed beside her on the bed and pressed his lips to hers. His blue eyes glittered in the sunlight. "Are you worried that *I* might have regretted what happened?"

She look away, blushing furiously. "Maybe."

"I don't do anything that I'll regret later. I might make mistakes, or have to do things I don't want to, but I never regret them. What's the point?"

"Oh, so what happened last night could still be considered a mistake?"

Julian gave her a level stare. "I don't think that. You don't think that either. I think your nerves are getting the better of you, you ridiculous woman."

"I'm *not* ridiculous."

"Any person whose hair is eight feet long is ridiculous. It's a known fact."

Evie snickered at the comment despite herself. When Julian proffered her a bread roll she took it, though she had no appetite. She *was* nervous, after all. Today was the day: the day she was to be reunited with her family, took her place as princess and finally found out what had happened that resulted in her being sent to live in isolation for twelve years.

She gulped. "Julian, I –"

"Don't talk," he said, before gently placing his fingertips to Evie's scalp and turning her head slightly away from him. "Just eat, and I'll fix your gigantic bird's nest of hair."

"It's not *my* fault it's such a mess," she muttered.

"I'd say we're jointly to blame. Now sit still."

And so Evie forced herself to eat whilst Julian reignited the enchantment on her hair he'd so eagerly unravelled the night before. She almost didn't want him to; it felt like he was eliminating the most obvious sign that, even if it was for but a few hours, Evie had been his.

She sighed, then frowned when she noticed there were no clothes lying on the floor. Julian was wearing his, looking just as heart-stoppingly handsome in the daylight as he had done in the darkness. "Where's my dress?" Evie asked, glancing behind her at Julian when he let go of her head.

"I folded it away," he explained. "I packed all of your

belongings up for you an hour or so ago, since you're so inept at it."

"I don't have *magic* to make all my clothes neat and tidy!"

"Do you honestly believe I use my powers for something so frivolous?"

Evie hesitated. "...yes?"

"On this one and only occasion you would be correct," he chuckled. "That blue dress was too large to fit in your bag, so I worked a spell into it so it could carry more. Now go back to your room and get dressed."

"I...do we really have to rush so quickly to the palace?" Evie asked, eyes downcast. She wasn't ready for this, even though it was all she'd ever wanted from the moment she was locked in the tower. But after experiencing what it was like to be an adult – to be free and happy and together with people instead of alone – Evie had to wonder if what she wanted had changed.

Julian kissed the top of her head. "I thought we might take a walk through the park first, then find somewhere to have lunch. Unless you'd rather not?"

"No, I'd love that!"

Pleased by the way Evie lit up at the idea, Julian held her hands and helped her from the bed. His eyes roved down her naked body, and he frowned slightly before

169

looking away.

"I'll go get your dress for you," he mumbled. Evie thought she could see Julian's cheeks beginning to flush as he stalked out of the room, and her heart leapt.

If I ever doubted he was attracted to me before, I don't now.

When Julian returned he was holding the elaborate cream gown embroidered with golden flowers that Evie had bought for today. The sleeves hung long and loose and translucent from her shoulders, and the skirt whispered along the floor. The tailor had wanted Evie to buy a hoop skirt but the sheer size of them, as well as the difficulty in wearing one, meant she had declined.

"You look like a princess," Julian said after he finished helping Evie button up the back of the dress. His tone was almost reverent; something about it unsettled her. But Evie waved away her concerns when he held out an arm, and she gladly took it. "Shall we pretend we're pompous aristocrats for the morning?"

Evie's lips quirked. "Isn't that technically what we both are?"

"Our *families* are. We're simply their no-good children benefiting from the wealth they amassed."

"Well if that's the case," she laughed, "then lead on, Julian."

170

*

Two hours later and Evie's stomach was rumbling loudly. Julian rolled his eyes as they wound their way through the park, though he stopped walking when they reached the midway point of a thick, ancient wooden bridge crossing the narrow point of a lake. Above them a massive, sweeping willow tree provided partial shade from the heat of the summer sun. Its leaves brushed across the top of Evie's hair, tickling her scalp.

"Are you wanting to eat?" Julian asked, sliding an arm around Evie's waist when a pair of well-dressed woman spied him from afar. It sent a small shiver of pleasure running down her spine to know that he was telling them he was hers, even if that would only remain true for another few hours.

She looked up at Julian, enthralled by the way the willow tree cast alternating strips of shadow and light rippling across his face. It was almost magical. "I can wait," Evie smiled, "if it means we get to spend a little longer here."

When Julian returned her smile it made her heart ache. Did she really have to say goodbye to him today? What was the protocol for princesses marrying wizards? Could she choose who she married?

Stop getting ahead of yourself, Evie, she scolded. Who was she to be thinking of marriage – least of all with

171

Julian – when she didn't even know what kind of welcome awaited her at the palace?

"Evie, I have a confession to make," Julian said, starkly bringing her out of her thoughts. There was something about the expression on his face that both excited and scared her.

Evie brushed her fingers against his arm. "What kind of confession?"

"I –"

"Do not take her to the palace!"

Evie didn't immediately turn to see who had interrupted her conversation with Julian. Rather, she watched in growing concern as Julian's irises began to glow, and his hands clenched into fists by his sides.

"I told you to leave us alone, old man," he muttered.

"You think I can allow my daughter to walk right into a trap?!"

It was this comment that made Evie turn, and when she did her heart stopped for an achingly long moment.

"Uncle...?" she whispered, barely able to comprehend the sight of the man standing before her. He was greying at the temples where his hair had once been golden, and his face was far more lined that Evie remembered it being, but it was her uncle Francis nonetheless.

He called me his –

"Julian, what's going on?" she asked, alternating between glancing at him and her uncle. "You know my uncle? What's –"

"Genevieve, please," Francis pleaded. "There isn't time. You must get away from Willow as fast as you can."

"Why did you call me your daughter? What's going on? Why must I leave?"

Francis glared at Julian. "If you had taken her away when I asked you to there would be all the time in the world to explain everything to her!"

Evie frowned. "Julian, what is he saying? What do you know that I don't?"

The wizard was agitated and angry. He took hold of Evie's hand, insistently pulling her closer to him. "I'm not taking her to the palace but nor am I letting you or the rest of your family near her."

"Wait, what?!" Evie tried to yank her hand away from Julian's and failed; he was too strong. She turned to her uncle. "What's going on here? Someone explain it to me *now.*"

Francis took a step towards her. "Genevieve, the king is not your father. Your mother and I – we – we loved each other for a long time. We hadn't meant for things to end up like this. We –"

173

"No," Evie mouthed. She didn't want to believe what she was hearing. If the king was not her father, and the king had found out, then...

I was sent to the tower because I'm not his daughter. I thought he loved me, like I loved him.

"It's true," her uncle said, shaking his head miserably. "I wish you weren't finding out like this. But my brother is *looking* for you; he's been looking for you since you disappeared from the tower. If you go to him now nothing good will come of it."

Evie's eyes darted towards Julian, whose face bore an agonised expression. "And you...knew? You knew this whole time yet you didn't tell me? Even though it was about *me*? And now you're saying you were never going to take me to the palace anyway? So why are we here? Why –"

"Evie, let me explain –"

"No!" she cried, and this time she managed to wrench herself away from Julian. "No. I don't want to hear it." She looked at her uncle. "Both of you could have told me the truth whenever you wanted. You could have kept me involved so I didn't feel so in the dark about my own life." Evie laughed bitterly. "Here I was longing for answers and you had them. You just didn't want to give them to me."

"Evie –"

174

"Genevieve –"

She ran from both Julian and her uncle. Blinded by tears, barely comprehending where she was going, and not caring if they were following, she ran. Concerned bystanders held out their hands as if to help but Evie ran past them all, too. It was too much. She couldn't trust anyone.

Julian had lied to her for god knows how long, and yet she had trusted him anyway because she had nobody else *to* trust.

I was a fool. A hopeless, naïve fool.

When Evie crashed into the broad chest of a stranger she stumbled back and stuttered her apologies. She didn't expect him to grab her arm in a crushing grip. "Please, sir, I didn't mean to hit you," she babbled wildly. When Evie looked up she realised the man was a soldier.

"I'm here to escort you to the palace, Princess Genevieve," he said, face flat and impassive in a way only a soldier's could be.

"I – I don't want to –"

His grip tightened. "That wasn't a request."

Upon looking around Evie realised there were at least five additional soldiers of a lower rank than the one holding her, as well as a man in fine clothing who was looking around for something – or someone.

175

"Thorne is close by," he said. "I can feel his magic."

Evie felt her insides turn to ice. *Thorne? Wasn't that the name people called the wizard who worked for my father – the king? Just how involved is Julian in what happened to me?*

"Leave him for now," the man whose hand was crushing Evie's forearm ordered. "We have the princess; we don't need him."

Evie numbly allowed the soldiers to escort her to the palace, though it was now the last place on earth that she wanted to go to. All she could think about was what Julian had told her that night in the tent, when Evie realised she'd fallen for him.

She'd known him well enough, he'd said. Well enough.

For Julian, 'well enough' meant Evie had known him precisely not at all.

CHAPTER EIGHTEEN

Julian

"You just couldn't leave us alone, could you?" Julian seethed. "Everything was going fine until you showed up!"

Francis stared at him in disbelief. "Until *yesterday* it seemed as if you intended to take Genevieve to the king! What was I supposed to do?"

"You think I couldn't have protected Evie if something went awry at the palace? The last time I checked the only wizard in the country better at transportation magic than I am is my father, and he's *dead.*"

When the other man flinched Julian became certain that Francis had been keeping some hugely important secret from the beginning. He was furious. *If I'd had every piece of information then I could have made the right call much earlier than this!* Julian thought, though such a belief was tainted by the knowledge that he'd so easily done to Evie what Francis had done to him.

Julian closed the gap between them. To Francis' credit he didn't back away, though Julian's entire frame was rippling with magic. "Tell me what it is you don't want me to know. Tell me what it is, then I'll take Evie and get her away from all of this."

Francis shook his head. "No, find Genevieve first and –"

"She's fifty metres that way," Julian interrupted, pointing to his left. "There's no 'finding' necessary."

"...you cast a tracking spell on her?"

"Of course I did. Do you take me for a fool?"

Francis frowned. "Does she know?"

"What do *you* think? Now tell me what it is you're hiding from me before I blast your head off."

"You said something similar to me before," Francis murmured, "but I know you wouldn't do anything of the sort, Julian."

Julian's fury only grew. "And why do you *know* such a thing, old man?"

"Because your father told me. He said you had always been gentle – that combative magic hadn't come easy to you as a child, because you preferred not to fight. It's how I knew I could trust you with such dangerous powers around my daughter."

"I'm not who I was as a child," Julian laughed derisively. "Having my father mysteriously die changed things, unsurprisingly."

"Julian, he isn't dead."

"He – what?"

The two men stared at each other in silence for a few moments, though the air crackled with sparks and bolts of magic. Julian could barely suppress it anymore; after everything that had transpired over the past month it threatened to consume him.

My father told me that's why one needed a strong mind to control it, he thought numbly. *He said I wasn't suited for such aggressive magic. Clearly he was right, though I've been desperate to prove him wrong. For the past twelve years all I've wanted to do is show a* dead man *that I can do all the things he could do.*

But now Francis Saule, the king's brother, was telling Julian his father was very much alive.

"If he's alive why haven't I heard from him?" Julian asked, voice clipped and very, very quiet. "If he's alive then why is it that only *you* know that he is?"

Francis shook his head. "I'm not the only one who knows – I'm merely the only one who isn't confined to the palace. Julian, I told you before that your father was the one who sent Genevieve to Thorne tower, but I didn't tell you the truth of *why* he did so."

"So tell me now, and I can be on my way."

The older man darted his eyes back and forth as if checking they weren't being listened to. At this point Julian couldn't care less if they were or not.

"Jacques knew about me and Mariette," Francis explained. "He didn't approve of what we were doing but the country was stable and safe only because we were around to temper my brother's selfishness. Jacques knew that too many would suffer if he said anything to the king, so he kept quiet."

"But then Pierre found out anyway," he continued, voice getting faster with every word as if he was expecting to be caught by an invisible hand at any moment. "He found out about what Mariette and I were doing – that we'd been together for years. He found out about Genevieve. And...he found out that your father had known about it, and hadn't told him."

"Pierre didn't want the country – or neighbouring

kingdoms – to know of his humiliation. What did it say of a king when those closest to him all betrayed him? So instead of killing us for our treasons he punished us in different ways. He shamed me as a war criminal and exiled me from the country. He imprisoned Mariette in the palace, preventing her from going out and helping those most in need as she had always done. He sent Genevieve away, since he couldn't bear to look at her. And then, since *he* had lost a child, he forced the same fate upon your father."

Julian struggled to comprehend what he was being told. "I am still alive," he said. "There was never an attempt on my life. So what –"

"My brother reasoned that if he *actually* killed you then he could never force Jacques to continue working for him," Francis interrupted. "And so he imprisoned your father in the palace as he had done with Mariette, upon pain of death to his son if he didn't do everything he ordered."

"...did that include sending food and other supplies to Evie in the tower?" Julian asked, thinking about how half-starved she'd been when he first met her.

Francis nodded. "Going by how small Genevieve was a month ago I can only conclude that my brother didn't want her to grow strong. Another punishment for me and Mariette, I suppose, for us to suffer knowing our daughter wasn't being –"

"*Evie was the one who suffered*," Julian corrected, his fury rediscovered on her behalf. "You talk about how this person was punished and that person was punished but you were all guilty! You deserved to be punished! But Evie is innocent; so innocent, in fact, that the only thing she wanted to do was to be reunited with the family responsible for ruining her life!"

"Julian, I –"

"Why did you keep the information about my father to yourself?" he cut in, not interested in the man's apologies. All he needed was an answer to that one question, then Julian could be done. He'd grab Evie, disappear with her, then apologise to her until the end of time if need be.

Francis sighed. "Because you would have gone to the palace immediately to seek your father out, instead of keeping Evie safe. Jacques and I had been in contact all these years through a long-running channel he'd used his magic to set up back in the war, so when you appeared in the tower he informed me of your arrival immediately. As it happened, I'd spent months sneaking back into the country and working out how to breach the tower. I was surprised by my luck in having the solution to getting Evie out of the damn thing literally appearing out of thin air."

"When I met you on the road – when I watched as, instead of burning those men intent on harming my daughter, you stunned them – I saw with my own eyes what Jacques had always told me: that you were gentle at heart. But I also saw just how strong you were. Even the gentlest soul can break, Julian, and your weak point is your family just as it is Genevieve's. You would ignore her wellbeing in favour of saving your father, and –

"Don't talk as if you know me!" Julian yelled. He sent a wicked blade of heat out towards Francis, smothering the magic entirely the moment before it would have obliterated him. "You think I'd so easily put Evie in danger after saving her life? After looking after her? I *love* her, damn it!"

He didn't know where the words had come from but if Julian had spoken them then he knew they must be true. It was liberating in a bizarre, twisted way, to realise the extent of his affection for Evie mere moments after potentially ruining their relationship forever.

But Francis shook his head sadly. "You don't love her, Julian. You love that she relies on you, and that she gives your life purpose. After spending thirteen years aimlessly travelling all alone, how could you not?"

"Don't tell me –"

"If you loved her you wouldn't have kept her in the dark about why she was sent to the tower after I told you," Francis cut in. His eyes were hard; his mouth set in a tight line. "Even now, you're not doing what's best for Genevieve. You should have run after her and told her

183

everything she wanted to know. Instead, you're so obsessed with getting the answers *you* need that you've thrown her wellbeing to the side."

Julian hated being called out on his behaviour like that. Who was this man – who was responsible for what happened to Evie in the first instance – to tell him whether his own feelings were genuine or not? But then he became aware of another feeling that turned his bones to ice.

Julian could no longer feel his connection to Evie.

With a snap of his fingers Julian transported to the last place she'd been before his magic was snuffed out. He found himself standing on a paved road that led out through the park towards the river, but Evie was nowhere to be seen. Out of the corner of his eye Julian saw a group of soldiers pointing and running towards him, so with a curse he once more clicked his fingers and disappeared right out of the city.

Back to Thorne tower.

He stared at his trembling hands with eyes gone blind with panic and horror.

"...what have I done?"

CHAPTER NINETEEN

Genevieve

When Evie was brought through the ornate palace gates, across the handsome paved courtyard and into the palace itself, all she could think of was how stupid she'd been to have ever believed her return to Willow would be a joyful one.

Never mind the fact Julian should have told me what he knew, she thought, *I should have been far more suspicious about the reason I was sent to the tower in the first place. I should have searched for answers before I came anywhere close to the palace.*

But it was too late now. Come hell or high water Evie

had returned home. Alone. She could only hope her world wouldn't come crashing down around her more than it already had done.

It was only once she was escorted to the doors of the throne room that the soldier holding her arm finally let go. She massaged the area immediately, wincing at the pain he'd caused. Evie knew that, in a few hours, there would be bruises where the man's fingers had been.

"Your father will see you now," he said, before unceremoniously pushing Evie through the doors once they'd been opened for her.

If everything miraculously works out okay then I'm going to strip him of his job, Evie decided, though she could have laughed at so ridiculous a notion as 'everything working out'. Nothing was going to work out the way she wanted it to, and she knew it.

"Genevieve."

As soon as she heard her name Evie stopped thinking at all. She slowed to a stop several feet from the throne she used to sit on as a child, back when she played at being queen when her father was busy. The marbled floor beneath her was polished to such a high shine Evie could vaguely see her reflection in it; her face was painted with fear and trepidation. But she couldn't look at the floor.

She had to look up.

"Father," she said, voice coming out as barely a whisper. Evie gulped, and tried again, this time bowing her head slightly as she spoke. "Father. I don't know what to – it's so good to see you."

The worst part was that, despite everything she'd learned today, Evie wasn't lying. The man sitting on the throne was older than he was in her memories, but time had not been as unkind to him as it had been his brother. King Pierre's hair was still sun-gold all the way through, and the lines on his handsome face made him look regal instead of worn and tired. Evie's heart hurt to see him in a powder blue jacket and waistcoat similar to the ones he'd so frequently worn when she was a child – the reason she loved the colour so much.

When he smiled Evie couldn't help but return it. "My love," he said. "My beautiful Genevieve. Look how much you've grown. You are my spitting image."

The words felt wrong to Evie's ears, perhaps because she was now aware that the man in front of her wasn't actually her father, and he knew he wasn't, too. But he did not necessarily know that *she* knew. Perhaps her fate might not be as bad as Francis feared.

"I've missed you," she said. "How I've missed you and mama. Where is she? Can I see her?"

"We've been reunited for less than one minute and you want to see *her*?" the king spat, his previous loveliness gone as if it had never existed. "That whore

187

who spent more time travelling the country than looking after her own child? You want to see her so badly even after all that?"

Evie said nothing. The king was testing her, she realised, to see if she knew about her true parentage. But it was only in her silence that Evie worked out that she'd failed the test. She cursed silently at her own stupidity. *I should have defended her,* Evie thought, as she watched the king's mouth contort into an ugly, satisfied snarl.

"I see your *real father* found you before I did. Tell me, Genevieve, how did you escape the tower?"

Evie tried to think on her feet as fast as she could, for if the king was asking how she did it then it was possible that she might be able to protect Julian. Though the wizard had lied to her – had concealed the truth from her at every opportunity – he had still saved her life several times. She didn't want the king to catch him.

"I climbed out," she said, allowing a flash of pride to cross her eyes. "I learned how to make a rope from a book in the tower, and turned every piece of clothing I was sent into another part of it. Eventually I made one long enough to escape."

The king raised a sceptical eyebrow. "You were strong enough to do such a thing?"

"I think desperation makes a person far stronger than they might otherwise be."

To Evie's complete surprise, he laughed. Her 'father' laughed, and it was loud and pleased and genuine. It left her feeling utterly confused.

He curled a finger towards her, motioning for Evie to come closer. She complied, walking onto the dais the throne sat on until she stood directly in front of her father. She kept her head held high. "Perhaps I should have listened to Thorne sooner," he said, casting a critical eye over her as he did so. "Clearly you are still my daughter in spirit if not in blood."

"So why send me away at all?" Evie demanded, realising that the best way to get answers was not to simper and fawn over the king but to instead face up to him directly, as he would have done. "Did you not love me? I didn't know what was going on. You are, and always will be, my father."

"Of course I loved you," he insisted. "You are the only one whom I *do* love. But what your mother did to me – what my own brother did to me – was inexcusable. They had to be punished. Knowing you were locked up because of their own vile natures was the least I could do to ensure justice was served."

That's not love. That's not –

"I can see from your face what you're thinking, Genevieve," the king said, frowning. "You think that if I loved you I couldn't have done that. But some things are bigger than one person's love for another. But I'll

189

demonstrate my love for you now: you can spend the night with your witch of a mother, then tomorrow I will gladly present you to the people of Willow as the princess and heir to the throne you truly are."

Evie hesitated before asking her next question. "And what of my brother? I heard I have a –"

"A brother of no consequence," he sniped back. "Whose ungodly sick blood demonstrates just how ruinous your mother truly is." The smile he plastered on his face did absolutely nothing to hide the hatred and malice lurking in his eyes. He motioned to a guard by the door. "Take her to her mother. Genevieve, I shall see you tomorrow. I have a lot to prepare before then."

Evie could do nothing but allow herself to be swept down corridors she had once known so well. They were meticulously clean, and immaculately furnished, but she realised there was no love in the grand building she used to adore. She wondered if there had ever been.

I hardly got any answers to my questions, Evie thought sadly. *Though seeing how bitter and angry my father is I can understand why my uncle wanted me to stay away.* Evie froze for a moment when she remembered that, technically, her father was her uncle and vice-versa.

None of that matters. Nothing matters at all. I should never have –

190

"Evie."

It was different from hearing the king say her name. It was different from hearing her uncle say her name. The voice belonged to the one person Evie had longed to see above anyone else.

"Mama," Evie cried, tripping over her own feet in her haste to fall into the woman's arms. Her mother was sitting upright in her bed, supported by several pillows. When Evie bowled into her most of them fell to the floor, but neither of them cared.

"How I've missed you, Evie," her mother sobbed, tears falling from her eyes to land on Evie's forehead. They clung to each other desperately, as if at any moment either of them might be taken away forever.

"I love you," Evie said, over and over again until her mother must surely have grown tired of hearing the words. Instead she merely said them right back until, eventually, she placed a gentle finger below Evie's chin and lifted her face.

"How beautiful you have become," she said. "And your hair – what is in your hair? It's the loveliest thing I've ever seen."

"...magic," Evie said, though something had felt different about it ever since she'd been caught by the soldiers. Something off. "I think I might like to brush it out, though, if you wanted to help me?"

Her mother broke out into a fresh sob, voice cracking even as she smiled and said, "Yes. Yes, of course, my beautiful little girl."

But as Queen Mariette pulled out the golden comb and baby-soft brush that had been stored away for twelve years and began unravelling Evie's countless braids, part of her daughter sincerely wished to jerk away from her touch. For so long as magic remained within every strand Evie's hair belonged as much to someone else as it did to her.

Julian, she thought, though she didn't want to think of him at all. *You no-good, lying, heart-breaking wizard.* Evie wanted him to leave Willow and never come back, so that her father would never find him and Evie herself would never have to see him again. But it was hopeless to think such a thing, because of course she wanted to see Julian again, even just once.

We never got to say goodbye.

CHAPTER TWENTY

Julian

Evie is in the palace.

My father is in the palace.

Evie is a prisoner in the palace.

My father is a prisoner in the palace.

Evie is –

Julian loosed a blast of magic at the old, rickety bed that still smelled so much of her. It exploded into pieces, driving large wooden shards and splinters into books and walls and Julian's flesh alike, knocking him unconscious.

When he woke, hours later, the sky was dark outside the tower's window. Julian cursed as he struggled to sit up, groggily sending out a pulse of magic from within his very core to drive out the wooden stakes that had lodged themselves in him. He didn't want to stop the bleeding they'd caused even as he resigned himself to doing exactly that, feeling as if he deserved each and every wound he'd inflicted upon himself. He deserved so much worse.

Evie had been taken away and it was all his fault.

Julian knew he should never have stood there arguing with Francis for so long. Had he immediately gone after Evie and spirited her away with him he could easily have located the man at a later, much safer, time and gotten the answers from him that Julian badly needed. The problem was that Francis himself had been right: Julian should have been honest with Evie from the very moment he'd found out about her true parentage. Had he done so then the past few hours might never have happened.

"So why didn't he *tell her himself*?!" Julian demanded to the empty air of the tower. "Why did he leave it to me to tell Evie about *his* mistakes?"

He couldn't understand it. What had Francis hoped would happen by entrusting the fate of his daughter to Jacques Thorne's son? Why *had* he entrusted Evie to Julian? He'd said he was planning to help Evie escape himself.

Had he explained who he was on the road then Evie could have chosen to go with her uncle instead of me. Or her father. Whoever he is. Or we could have all travelled together.

Julian thought back over the past month he'd spent with Evie. Days and weeks of her incessant chatter and disgusting naïvety and insatiable curiosity, driving him to the point of madness on more than one occasion. But it was *Julian* she had bothered with everything she wanted to know, or wanted him to know. *Julian* whom she spoke to about the food she'd tried for the first time that day, or the heron she saw fishing in a river, or the shooting star she'd thought was falling from the sky.

If Francis had been there things would have been very, very different.

Was he right to say I don't truly love her? Who is he to deny my feelings when I've only just worked out what they are?

Julian kicked the windowsill. Nobody had the right to tell him what he did or didn't feel, or what he should or shouldn't do. He'd gotten by just fine acting on his own impulses; listening to his own morality. By and large Julian was a good man, even if he was grumpy and quick to irritate. He helped people. He saved princesses from towers and brigands and leering boys and guided them all the way back home.

"And bedded them in the process," he muttered, chuckling darkly. He really had messed everything up. But who else but Julian himself could fix things? He certainly wasn't going to rely on Francis, who up until this point had only made things worse.

With a grim smile Julian waved a hand at the floor. The wooden panelling opened up to reveal a helical stairway, which he promptly descended.

How Evie would cry in frustration if she knew this had been here all along, Julian thought, amused despite himself when he reached the bottom of the tower. There were several rooms and stores down here which contained a multitude of magical tomes and spells and both dangerous and wondrous elixirs. Julian ignored them all, choosing instead to venture into another room full of fabric.

"You really do have a flair for good clothes, father," Julian mused as he browsed through the man's expansive selection. "So what outfit would Evie like the most...?"

In the end Julian chose a deep red waistcoat with the suggestion of flames embroidered into the fabric with burgundy thread, and a pair of tan trousers with polished ebony buttons. They paired well with dark boots and a white shirt, which meant all Julian had left to select was an overcoat.

Or a cloak, he thought, grinning when he spied one made of a thick, lush fabric the colour of wine. It was so expansive that Julian imagined enveloping Evie within it, holding her against him as he kissed her until they both couldn't think of anything else but each other.

When he finished selecting clothes Julian headed back upstairs to the small bathroom Evie had used for twelve years. There was no water to be seen, so Julian focused his magic outdoors and redirected some from a stream through the tower's window into the old, rusted iron tub. He didn't bother heating it up, instead relishing in the nip of cold water on his skin as he washed his own blood from his skin. After that Julian shaved his face and cleaned his hair, smoothing it back the way his father had always worn it.

Julian glanced outside. His fire magic would be stronger when the sun was up. Though he was antsy and impatient to do something *now,* it was better to wait. Just another few hours and he could be on his way. So Julian set about cleaning the mess he'd left of the tower after he'd exploded the bed, then searched through some of his father's books until he found the transfiguration spells he'd need to conjure up a new one.

It kept him busy enough, though Julian's thoughts were constantly on Evie. What kind of bed would *she* like? Something grand? Something modest? Something made of beech or maple or cherry wood? Iron? In the end Julian made a sturdy oak four-poster bed with curtains to keep out the morning sun, which at this point had flooded the tower.

Julian grinned as he felt it heat up his skin. He could do his best – or worst – magic now. He retrieved the clothes he'd chosen from his father's store then, with adrenaline-shaking hands, carefully put them on. When he was done Julian hardened a layer of air in front of him to turn it into a mirror to inspect his reflection.

He frowned at the person he saw. Just two days ago Julian had thought he looked like his father – except for his eyes. Blue eyes. His mother's eyes. Gentle eyes that meant Julian didn't have the heart to use the powerful, fiery magic within him to its fullest potential.

"We'll see about that," Julian announced in challenge, fastening his cloak with one final glance out through the tower window. A challenge to the king, who didn't know what he could do. A challenge to his father, who had always thought his gentleness a flaw. A challenge to Francis, who was convinced Julian would only use such devastating power for his blood-related family.

And a challenge to himself, to prove them all wrong.

"I'm coming for you, Evie," Julian said, and then he was gone.

CHAPTER TWENTY-ONE

Genevieve

If somebody had asked Genevieve what she thought she'd be doing that morning it was not having breakfast at a solemn dining table with her father, her mother, and a hunched-over, greying man she did not recognise.

"Did you sleep well, Genevieve?" her father asked, all sweet smiles and false politeness as he began eating. He deliberately avoided casting his gaze over anyone but her, which raised the question: why were her mother and the stranger there at all?

"I – well, father," Evie replied. "I slept well, thank you." She glanced to her left; her mother was picking away at her plate of food listlessly. In the bright morning light Evie could see how frail she'd gotten, as if a stiff wind might blow her away. Now, for all intents and purposes, it seemed as if the queen had been the one locked in a tower whilst Evie had been free to eat as she pleased.

Evie didn't like it. Though her mother had indeed betrayed the king alongside his brother, she had been the one to bear the worse fate of the two.

At least my uncle got to roam free, she thought, *though I suppose for him the worst part of his punishment was no longer being able to rule the country fairly in place of the king. Or maybe being separated from my mother was the worst part.*

Evie had to admit she didn't know the adults around her nearly as well as she needed to. When she was a child she'd loved them all regardless of their temperament, or the secrets they held, or the way they punished others. Dully she thought of Julian, whom she thought she *had* known.

And look where that got me. Clearly I'm not cut out for understanding people.

"Ah, if only my brother were here," the king opined, sighing dramatically. "Then we'd have the whole, happy family back together. Wouldn't that be wonderful, Mariette? You could continue fucking him behind my back and laughing at my ignorance, all the while handing me bastard children with a treacherous smile on your face!"

Mariette flinched at her husband's words, though she stayed silent. Evie didn't think she'd have been able to do the same if anybody spoke to *her* like that. She had to wonder where her mother's backbone had gone – had her imprisonment truly broken her? Evie had been locked up as long as she had, after all, and she certainly wasn't ready to give up on the life she wanted just yet.

It's simply a case of whether I can grab it, she thought, watching her father with careful eyes as she did so. *He says he's going to make me his heir. Do I even want that? Did I ever want the throne, aside from when I played games of make-believe as a child? Considering how poorly I have judged people thus far I somehow doubt I'd be any good at it. But then again...*

"We'll have to get you some new clothes, Genevieve," her father said, pointing distastefully at her dress. "What you have on is much too common. It sickens me to see you debase yourself so."

Evie was wearing the dark green dress Julian had paid for the day they first slept in the tent together. She loved it dearly, despite the pain thinking of Julian caused her. Her father hated it because it was 'too common', though it was beautiful and well-made. He really didn't care for anyone living outside of Willow – anyone with real problems living on a pittance in villages in desperate need of help.

I could not be worse than my father at ruling, though that doesn't exactly set the bar very high.

"Forgive me, father; I did not have the resources to procure fine clothing on my journey home," Evie said, wording her sentence as carefully as possible. *Never mention Julian. Never mention getting help at all.*

Evie knew Julian had been worried someone was tracking his magic; he never told her why. If the king already knew about him and had someone tracking him Evie could do nothing to help him, though if she denied having any aid from him whatsoever regarding her escape from the tower then perhaps, even if he *was* caught, Julian would receive no punishment. It was the best outcome Evie could hope for.

"You'll need never have to worry about such things again, my daughter," the king said. He poured himself a cup of pale, golden wine, and then another for Evie, and then – to her surprise – one for her mother and one for the unmoving, greying statue of a man sitting to the right of Evie. When the king indicated for them to pick up the drinks she watched the old man slowly reach a shaking hand out for his. She wondered if he was strong enough to hold it.

"A toast to the palace, and to our *family*," her father announced. "May we –"

"Mama?"

Evie turned her head to stare at the entrance to the dining hall. There stood a small, golden-haired boy around the age she'd been when she was sent to the tower. His large, green eyes stood out in stark contrast against his pale and sickly skin. He coughed several times into his hands; when he pulled them away there was blood on his fingers.

The king wrinkled his nose in distaste. "Get him away before he makes us all sick," he ordered the woman who frantically appeared in the doorway a second later. "I told you to keep him away from –"

"Louis? Are you Louis?" Evie asked, ignoring her father completely.

The boy's eyes grew even wider when they spied her. "That's my name. Who are you? You look like me."

"I'm your sister." She smiled gently. "I have been gone for a long time, but now I'm back. Won't you come in so I can greet you properly?"

"Genevieve, don't touch him," her father said. "He is full to the brim with disease. It won't be good for you to get close."

"If he's spent this long in the palace without getting anyone else sick I somehow doubt he's contagious," Evie fired back, remembering one of several books on medicine she'd read back in the tower. "And I think I'd

203

like to meet my brother, all things considered."

This time the king kept his opinions to himself. Evie knew she was treading a fine line right now, hoping that her father's wish to 'demonstrate his love' for her would last just a little while longer. She waved Louis over and, with small, uncertain steps, he made his way over to her. When he reached her chair Evie swept him up into her lap, and he laughed in surprise.

"Much better," Evie said happily. She reached for some toast. "Are you hungry, little brother? You look like you could eat a horse."

Louis nodded, immediately enamoured with this new sister of his who was unafraid to touch him, stood up to his father and offered him breakfast. He took the toast in his bloodied hands and eagerly wolfed it down.

Out of the corner of her eye Evie saw that her mother was watching the pair of them with the oddest expression on her face. It was torn between happiness and the deepest, darkest sadness, and it was only then that the extent of Louis' condition truly set in.

He is going to die soon, Evie realised with certainty. *His poor health has not been an exaggeration. He is doomed.* It was the worst situation imaginable in which to meet the other victim of the Saule family, and her only sibling.

"Your hair is very long," Louis said around a

mouthful of toast, casting his eyes down to the floor where Evie's hair pooled beneath her.

She laughed. "Yes, well, I didn't have anything with which to cut it where I was staying."

"Do you want to cut it?"

"Maybe one day," she said. "One day. Some day. We'll see."

The look her father gave her suggested he wanted it to be sooner rather than later.

"Louis, would you like some cheese?" she asked her brother, ignoring her father's looks as she reached out a hand to grab a platter full of the stuff. But her hand glanced against the edge of a sharp knife set beside it, slicing open her skin. Evie recoiled, wincing at the pain. "Guess I could cut my hair with that," she joked, to which her brother giggled.

The old, silent man to Evie's right held out a napkin to her. His trembling fingers touched the cut on her hand for but half a moment as she gratefully took it from him.

His trembling stopped.

"What is it, Thorne?" the king demanded, immediately aware that something was wrong. Evie stared at the man in horror – *this* was what remained of The Thorn Wizard? And then it hit her, though she should have worked it out a time ago.

The man was Julian's father.

Oh, Julian, she thought sadly. *Do you know he's here? You told me he was dead. Is this the reason you didn't want to tell me anything you knew? Is this –*

"Your Majesty," the man croaked. He finally looked up, pushing his hair out of his eyes in an achingly familiar gesture. And though his face was severely lined and gaunt from his imprisonment, and though his eyes were brown instead of blue, there was no doubt that this man was indeed Julian's father. "Princess Genevieve really *is* your daughter."

The king froze. "...what did you say?"

"Her blood," the wizard said, holding up his hand to show where he'd grazed past Evie's cut, "her blood does not match your brother'. It matches yours."

Both Evie and her father darted their eyes towards the queen. Her face was ashen; she was shaking.

"You *lied* to me about my own daughter?" the king seethed. He stood up in order to tower over her. "You had me believe all this time that –"

But then a rumbling in the corridor gave them all pause; even the king forgot what he was about to say. The rumbling got louder, and closer, until by the time it reached the dining room it was a dull roar. There was a crackling to it, too.

Like fire.

"Julian," Evie whispered, a split second before the man himself appeared through the doorway, surrounded by flames and seemingly dressed in them, too. His eyes were murderous coals. He raised a hand to point at Evie.

"I'll be taking her with me."

CHAPTER TWENTY-TWO

Julian

"Julian!"

Evie's voice cut through the commotion all around him like an arrow to the heart. Julian locked eyes with her, the ghost of a grin upon his lips before he turned to snarl at the king.

"After sending her away you have no right to have her by your side. I'm leaving with her whether you like it or not."

It took the king a few moments to regain his composure. After all, a man enveloped in fire was not a common sight. But then he looked closer at who the man in question was, and smiled. "You must be Thorne's boy. Nice to see you following in his footsteps so perfectly. You even walked yourself right into the palace for me. So obedient."

"I'm here for *her* and to save my father," Julian said through gritted teeth. "Where is he?"

The king gestured to an old man on his left whom Julian had admittedly not taken notice of yet. But now the old man was staring at him, and –

"Father."

Jacques Thorne nodded, his eyes bright as they took in the sight of his fiery, furious son. Julian was horrified by how old and gaunt he was; clearly Evie hadn't been the only one who'd been starving for twelve years. Forcing his gaze away from his father Julian realised that the queen, too, was looking just as frail, and the boy Evie had clutched to her chest wasn't doing well either.

In contrast Evie herself looked healthier than she'd ever been, tearing Julian's heart up as he thought about each and every pastry and pie and apple he'd complained about having to pay for on her behalf.

And then there was the king, resplendent in his finery and looking younger than his years. He was vicious and golden as a lion, standing to face off against Julian as if he didn't have a care in the world. His eyes gleamed as they took in the sheer power emanating off his adversary.

"You don't scare me with your magic, wizard," he said. "If you meant to do me harm you'd have done it already. So you want my daughter and your father? Well, how about you stay and work for me instead? Lord knows your father is well past his prime. Let him enjoy his retirement. I think that's a more than fair deal."

"There's nothing *fair* about what you inflicted upon him."

"Oh, so the fact he kept my wife and brother's treachery from me for years didn't deserve punishment? He – quiet, Louis!" he screamed at the small child sitting on Evie's lap, who had begun to sob. He only cried harder, so Evie wrapped her arms around him and stroked his hair until he quietened down.

For a moment Julian forgot to be angry, so enthralled as he was with the sight of Evie being gentle and kind in amongst the chaos surrounding her. *She is too good for them all,* he thought, casting his gaze around the room. *Her father, mother, uncle. All of them.*

Julian glared at the king. "I don't care for the transgressions of the past. I'm taking my father, and I'm taking Evie, and you aren't going to stop me."

"You're a confident one, aren't you?" he laughed. Pierre moved around the table, stopping by Julian's father. He put a hand on his shoulder. "But you are not the king, boy; *I* am. And as a subject of this country you must do as I say. And if you continue to refuse, well..."

The king left his threat hanging obvious and ominous in the air. Julian faltered for but half a moment, then sent a strike of magic towards the dining table, sending it up in flames. Mariette, Evie and Louis recoiled from the heat immediately; Julian's father did not. Their magic could never hurt each other.

But Pierre acted as if nothing was wrong. "You know, wizard, your father discovered something very interesting not one moment before you showed up. Did you know the beautiful Genevieve really *is* my daughter? In name and in blood, she is mine. Do you really think that, after finding this out, I would so easily hand her over to the likes of you?"

Julian glanced at Evie, who nodded silently. Her long hair was no longer imbued with magic, hanging all the way down like a coil of gold to the floor. Her brother clung to it desperately, as if it would protect him from the flames.

"I don't care about her parentage," Julian said. "I never have. She could be a peasant for all I care."

"Ah, but she's not, and it matters. Stay here and work for me, Julian Thorne, or face the consequences. This is your last chance to obey my orders."

The two men stared at each other for what felt like

eternity. The table collapsed in on itself, smouldering to ashes upon the marble floor. Nobody dared say a word; all eyes were on Julian.

"I'm taking Evie," Julian finally said, just as the king pulled a blade from his sleeve and slashed his father's neck open from ear to ear.

"*Go,*" the dying man mouthed at his son, who stared in horror and disbelief as his father's life drained away before his very eyes. With no time left to think, Julian grabbed Evie's hair from the floor and snapped his fingers, barely aware of her cry of shock as his magic pulled them back to Thorne tower.

My father was right all along, Julian thought numbly. *I did not have it in me to kill a man, even one as deplorable as the king. Now both of us must suffer for it.*

CHAPTER TWENTY-THREE

Genevieve

It took Evie several moments of heaving oxygen into her lungs and struggling through tears before she realised Julian had transported her back to Thorne tower.

"I – Louis!" she cried out, grasping at air where her brother had been. "Where's Louis? And my mother! My –"

"He killed him," Julian bit out, though going by the look on his face he had not meant to interrupt Evie. Rather, he was speaking to nobody in particular, his eyes caught somewhere between blue and yellow, glowing magic. When Julian collapsed to the floor the angry flames surrounding him dissipated in puffs of smoke which filtered out the window.

Evie scrabbled to her feet to reach him, all concerns for her family momentarily forgotten in the face of Julian's desolation. But she tripped up on her hair in the process, falling gracelessly even as Julian held out an arm to catch her and pull her beneath his thick, billowing cloak.

He rested his chin on top of Evie's head; she could feel the erratic beating of Julian's heart against her right down to her bones. "He killed him, Evie," he muttered. "Your father killed mine. He –"

"You couldn't have done anything to save him," Evie cried, though the words felt hollow.

Julian's arms tightened around her. "I should have killed the king first. The moment I stepped foot inside that room I should have set his heart on fire, if he had one to set fire to at all."

"You could never do something so brutal," she replied, burying her head against Julian's chest to hide her tears. "Never in a hundred years could you do something like that."

"And look where 'couldn't' got me. I regained and lost my father in the space of twenty-four hours. What cruel world tells a son his father is alive only to rip him away moments later?"

"A world where princesses get put in towers for twelve years when they did nothing wrong."

The two of them were silent then, until finally Julian's heart rate slowed back down to normal. Evie's, however, continued to flutter as fast as a hummingbird, filling her stomach with nerves and foreboding.

"I have to go back, Julian," she said, very quietly.

"No."

"Julian –"

"I just lost my father, Evie. I'm not letting you go, too."

Evie struggled against him, though Julian only tightened his grip on her until she could barely breathe. "I need to go back for my mother!" she barely managed to exclaim. "For my brother!"

"They're both as good as dead," he spat. "The king will murder them as he did my father, or he'll let them continue to waste away to nothing." Julian loosened his arms, allowing Evie to finally take a large gulp of much-needed air. He held her out in front of him, eyes wet with tears and blind to all reason. "Don't you see, Evie? It's all over for them. There's nothing for you to go back to the palace for. Stay here."

Evie shook her head. She clung to the front of Julian's waistcoat miserably even as his hands dropped

215

from her shoulders. "I need to save them. I need to do *something*. I can't stay here."

"...you would leave me?"

"Julian, you lied to me!" Evie cried, forcing her eyes back to his. Her previous fury at the man in front of her reignited as if he'd set her on fire himself. "You could have told me what was going on so many times, but you didn't. Why should I stay with you?"

He frowned. "I was trying to protect you. You idolised your family; I didn't want to ruin that for you."

"I'm an adult. I could have handled it."

"Could you?"

"Why do you keep underestimating me?!" Evie raged, banging her fists against Julian's chest in the process. "Do you really think a young girl sent to live alone with no explanation as to why – who survived half-starved for twelve years, who actively tried to escape her fate – wouldn't be able to *handle* knowing that the people responsible for her misery were her family?"

Julian's expression hardened. He laughed bitterly. "Well now you know. And what did it matter, anyway? Turns out your mother lied about who your father was all along! What a mess of a family. I hope the king is kicking himself for having sent you, his own daughter, away. I hope he –"

Evie slapped him. "You are grieving. You just lost what remained of your family. But that does *not* give you the right to say such things to me. Now let me go, Julian. Send me back to the palace."

"No."

"Julian!"

He ran a hand through Evie's hair, pulling her face closer to his. There was a shine to his eyes that had nothing to do with magic and everything to do with madness. "I'll get revenge against the king for both of us. Just let him come, and I'll obliterate him from the face of the planet. He'll never bother either of us again. We'll be free."

Julian kissed her, a desperate gesture that caused Evie to stumble backwards and fall to the floor. Julian followed her down; climbing on top of her and deepening the kiss even as she struggled against him.

"Julian," she cried, "stop it! Stop it!" Evie clawed at his clothes, trying to drag him off her, but it was only after she kicked him in the stomach that he recoiled enough for her to scramble free. Evie retreated to the other side of the room, clutching her arms around herself protectively.

Julian watched her from his position on the floor, expression all disbelief and incomprehension. It broke Evie's heart to see him so twisted. "Why are you refusing me?" he asked, genuinely hurt.

"Because so long as you forbid me from leaving then you're no different from my father," Evie told him. She ran to the bathroom and locked the door behind her, for all the good it would do.

I can't believe I ever thought for a moment I'd go to bed happy tonight, she thought miserably, crying for everything she had lost. Her mother. Her brother.

Julian.

CHAPTER TWENTY-FOUR

Julian

Almost a week had passed and Genevieve hadn't spoken aloud even once. Not once since she pushed Julian away from her and locked herself away in the bathroom. Evie had since resurfaced, of course, but she resolutely refused to look at or talk to or listen to Julian.

It didn't matter what he did – what food he brought to her, what baths he ran her, what blankets he wove out of thin air to accompany the bed he'd made with her in mind – Evie did not respond. And so Julian slept on the floor night after night, keeping a respectful distance away, believing that eventually Evie would see the folly of her

219

silence and come back to him.

For though Julian was sorry for the way he'd acted towards her he could not be sorry for refusing to let her leave the tower. Evie was blinded by her longing for a brother who was doomed to die, and a mother who would soon follow. A mother who lied about her affair, and Evie's true parentage, and was the reason Evie had suffered so much in the first place. Perhaps Julian *should* have told her about why she'd been sent to the tower weeks ago; that way, her annoyingly-insistent, naïve love for the woman might have died already.

Died like my father, with a knife through his throat, Julian thought darkly, once more returning to mull over the precise moment all life drained from the man's eyes entirely.

It was sunset outside, and the sky was bloody and brutal. Julian revelled in it, so he sat on the windowsill to watch the horizon grow darker and darker in parallel to his mood. *I should have killed the king where he stood. I shouldn't have listened to a word he said. That way my father would be alive and Evie would not hate me so.*

He glanced behind him; Evie lay unresponsive on the bed, the gauzy curtains partially obscuring her from view. Julian could just barely spy the ends of her golden hair splayed in a mess across the floor at the foot of the bed. Evie hadn't let him enchant it to keep it clean and out of the way.

She hadn't let him touch her at all.

A familiar twist of longing mixed with frustrated, unruly desire consumed Julian as he watched her. He wanted Evie. He wanted to hold her and have her cling to him, like she had done before. To beg Julian for more; more touches, more kisses, more pleasure. More of him. *All* of him.

Instead Evie wanted nothing, leaving Julian wanting everything.

She'll come around, he thought, shielding his eyes from the glare of the sun's dying rays. *She has to. Soon I'll correct my mistake and kill the king. For the first time in her life Evie will truly be free. She'll thank me then.*

Perhaps, had Julian not been so incandescent with rage on his father's behalf, he'd have been able to see just how wretchedly he was treating Evie. He'd see what he was doing to her, and let her go. But Julian *needed* the rage. He needed to cling to the belief that getting his revenge would make everything right once more, just as he wished to cling to Evie herself.

If he didn't have his rage then all he had was grief, and Julian didn't know how to deal with it. So he hid it away beneath layers and layers of fire, never to be felt again.

"Julian, let her go!"

Julian's ears pricked up at the voice. It was

infuriatingly familiar.

"Go away, you bastard," he threw down to Francis, who stood at the base of Thorne tower looking exhausted beyond belief. To have reached the tower from Willow in seven days meant the king's brother had likely not slept much at all since he set out.

Julian didn't care.

"The king and part of his army are on their way, you fool!" Francis yelled. "What did you think would happen by kidnapping Genevieve?"

"He killed my father!"

"Because you stormed into the palace *on fire.*"

"He meant to imprison me there in place of him!" Julian screamed back. "Do you really think I was going to let that happen?"

Francis shook his head in frustration. "Look at the mess you've caused, Julian. Stop trying to fight like you're the only one who's on your side. Had you told me your intention to take back your father and Genevieve I'd -"

"What? Snuck me in through a back door?" Julian sneered. "My plan would have worked, had I only killed the king in time."

"But you didn't." Francis' eyes were hard. "You didn't, and now your father is dead."

"You don't get to berate me for what I did wrong! Not when you and the queen are the reason all of this happened in the first place. Although, at this point I'd say it's largely the queen at fault."

"...what do you mean by that?" the man called out, though the wind took most of the volume away from his voice. When the words reached Julian's ears they were more like a whisper.

He bent low over the windowsill to grin like a madman; if he leant out any further then he would fall. "All this time Queen Mariette played everyone for a fool. You. My father. The king. Evie was *his* child the entire time, not yours! She was locked in this godforsaken tower for absolutely no reason at all!"

The look on Francis' face was terrible; Julian relished it. He wanted to inflict as much pain as possible on all those responsible for what happened to his father until everyone felt as wretched as him.

"You're lying," the man said.

"I'm not. It was the last thing my father found out before he was murdered. One wonders why the queen lied about such a thing. Do you have any ideas?"

There was a darkness to Francis' expression that had nothing to do with the murky blues and purples pervading the sunset sky. "You are trying to rile me up because you are angry. You're upset. You have every

223

right to be. But –"

"I'm not lying about Evie's parents," Julian cut in. "And I think you know that."

Francis hesitated before saying, "It doesn't matter who her father is."

"It sure as hell matters to Evie."

"Julian, let me up there," the man insisted, knocking upon the stone tower as if a door would somehow open in front of him. "We need to come up with a plan to combat my brother. You cannot face him alone."

"I can and I will!" Julian screamed back, though he knew he sounded like a petulant child. "I made the mistake of staying my hand before. I won't do the same next time."

And then he turned from the windowsill, though Francis called for Julian to come back. Then he called for Evie, begging for her to listen to him, but she did not rouse from the bed. Julian knew she was listening going by how still was; when Evie was actually asleep she tossed and turned, full of fitful nightmares.

Eventually Francis quietened down and, when Julian moved back over to the window, saw that he had retreated into the forest. Julian discovered he didn't feel particularly victorious about sending the man on his way.

I can't think of him now. The king is on his way. 1

have to be ready.

He took a few quiet steps over to the foot of the bed, watching Evie through the curtains. Julian wondered if she'd try to stop him, regardless of what the king had done to her and everyone else she loved. But he couldn't let such doubts stop him; it was much too late for that.

One way or another Julian Thorne was going to kill a king. He'd face the consequences of what came after when they happened. But as he watched Evie his resolve faltered. He'd done so much to her. Too much. She would hate him until the end of time, and Julian would deserve it.

He sat on the end of the bed.

"Evie."

CHAPTER TWENTY-FIVE

Genevieve

Of course Evie had heard Julian's conversation with Francis. The king and an entourage of soldiers were on their way to Thorne tower to defeat the wizard and rescue the princess.

I don't want rescued, Evie thought. *Not like this. But I don't want to stay trapped in the tower either. I want to save my mother and little Louis. I want –*

"Evie."

She didn't respond. Julian had tried to get her to talk for a week now, though not one of his attempts had worked. Her self-imposed silence made Evie feel like she was living in the tower alone, as she had done for most of her life. It didn't matter that the bed was large and comfortable now, or that she had hot water and all the food she could eat.

Evie was trapped. She was a prisoner and didn't know what to do to free herself.

"Evie, please. I know you heard your uncle."

When she felt Julian's weight on the bottom of the bed she just barely glanced over at him. He sat by her hair, twisting strands of it around his fingers. Enveloped by the curtains hanging around them, Evie felt very much like she and Julian were the only people left in the world.

"I'm going to kill your father," Julian said quietly, still twirling Evie's hair. "I have to."

"I know."

His eyes darted to hers in surprise; clearly Julian hadn't thought Evie would actually reply. He reached a hand out a few inches before bringing it back to his lap, as if he meant to touch her but thought better of it.

"You don't approve?"

"I know it must be done."

"But you wish it didn't?"

Evie buried her head in the pillow beneath her, then

227

sat up to face Julian. He ventured a little closer towards her.

"He means to allow my brother to die," she began, very slowly. "And my mother, too. He killed your father because you wouldn't bow down to his threats. He is callous and cruel and doesn't care for anyone who doesn't live outside of Willow. If he could be imprisoned then I'd want to go down that route, but he's marching to meet you with an army. I don't see what other choice you have but to kill him."

"Evie –"

"Would you send me back to the palace *now,* Julian?" she cut in. "My father isn't there. We could easily save my mother and Louis now. You know we could."

Julian's eyes shone in the darkness. He shook his head. "They are safer there for now. If we were to remove them from the palace word would reach the king about it. And then what would he do? At least we know what to expect if we remain here and wait for him."

Evie stayed silent. Julian had a point, but that didn't mean she had to like it. Especially not when his entire frame of mind was still bent and angry and riddled with grief. He wasn't himself when she needed him to be.

But then what did that say of *her?* Julian had needed her all week, and she had ignored him. He didn't know how to cope with the death of his father. He had nobody to help him, even though Evie was right there.

She reached out a hand, brushing her fingertips against Julian's arm. He watched her do so with an agonised expression.

"Do you remember the nightmare that woke you from your sleep at the inn?" he asked. All around them the air became just as oppressive as it had done on the night in question to which Julian was referring, and though the evening was hot Evie shuddered.

"What about it?" she replied. Julian closed the gap between them, sliding a careful hand through Evie's hair as his lips grazed her collarbone. He kissed the skin there, whisper-soft, then moved up her neck to her jawline, trailing kisses as he went. Evie drew in a breath and closed her eyes. "What about it, Julian?" she asked again.

When he pushed her down with the full weight of his body on hers Evie did not resist. "You didn't know the name of the tower," he said, while his hands made quick work of the buttons on Evie's underdress and his trousers. "You didn't know my family name, and yet you dreamed of thorns trapping you in here, digging into your skin and consuming you."

Julian's mouth found Evie's; she desperately reciprocated the kiss. She cupped her left hand to Julian's face, feeling the unmistakable dampness of tears upon her fingertips.

"Let me help you," she begged. "Don't go through all of this alone. Talk to me, Julian." When Evie locked eyes with him she saw that his were burning. She reached up and kissed them, one after the other, feeling Julian's wet lashes against her lips. "Let me help."

"I'm going to destroy you," he said, miserable even as his hands continued to rove across Evie's body. He didn't seem to realise she was responding in kind. "See what I've done to you already. I have to let you go."

"I won't go now."

"...why not?"

"Because you need me," Evie told him. She pushed Julian's hair out of his face and smiled. "You told me once that I'd forgotten what it was like to be looked after, and I said I sometimes thought the same about you. Now I believe that more than ever. So let me look after you, Julian, as you've looked after me."

Julian looked at her uncertainly. "Evie –"

"You won't destroy me," she assured, "and I think we both know you won't trap me anymore, either. So just...let me help you."

There were no words for a long time after that. The desperation in Julian's body as he touched and kissed and clung to Evie was all she needed to know what he was feeling. It filled every stolen breath of air he forced into his lungs, even as that desperation seamlessly turned into wild, fervent desire that left Evie gasping for more.

It was only when the pair of them had been reduced to an exhausted entanglement of limbs that Julian finally sobbed. He broke down against Evie's shoulder, his sweat-soaked skin shuddering alongside his cries.

"What do I do?" he whispered. "What do we do, Evie?"

"We end this," she said, before kissing Julian's forehead and wiping his tears away. "We end this, and move on."

CHAPTER TWENTY-SIX

Julian

"Did we really have to involve him, Evie?"

"To help us construct a plan to overthrow the king? Yes, Julian, I'd say it serves us well to have my uncle here."

Julian glared at the man in question, who was sitting cross-legged on the floor and glaring right back at him. "He has been less than useless so far. All he's done is make things worse."

"So you keep saying," Francis fired back, "yet it appears that *you* are the only one with a body count to your name."

"You –"

"Both of you, stop!" Evie begged. "Uncle, you said my father wasn't far behind you. When might we expect him?"

"By sunrise for sure," he said, still glaring at Julian. "Which is good for Julian's magic, I suppose. If he has the *heart* to use it."

"Julian being unable to kill a man is not a flaw, uncle."

"It is in this particular situation," Julian and Francis said in unison, which only served to further their dislike of each other.

Evie sighed. When she dragged her hand across her face in exasperation Julian burst out laughing; it was a gesture he was very familiar with, considering the numerous times he had done it in Evie's presence.

She frowned. "What is it?"

"I think you're beginning to understand what it's like to look after a brat," Julian explained, before sliding an arm around her and pulling her closer towards him. Evie blushed even as she rolled her eyes at Julian's insinuation.

Francis watched their interaction with disapproval. It only served to make Julian want to show off how close he and Evie were even more, but for her sake he resisted.

"It doesn't matter if Julian can't kill Pierre, anyway," Francis said, after a moment of crackling tension between the two of them.

Julian's eyes narrowed. "And why is that?"

"Because I'm going to take care of my brother personally. All you have to do is incapacitate his army so it'll be a fair fight."

"*You* will kill him?" Julian asked incredulously. To his left Evie let out a small gasp of surprise. "You're old and tired, Francis."

"Not so old and not so tired that I can't pierce my brother's heart with a sword or shoot him with a pistol," Francis said, smiling grimly. "I was a better swordsman than he was in the war, and he's grown slow and spoiled in the palace. He will not be able to beat me."

"And if he does?"

"Then I guess, for everyone's sake, you better set him alight this time."

Nobody said a word in response to Francis' jibe.

Hours later, after the sun had long since dipped below the forest, Julian and Evie lay huddled together, enjoying the breeze that came through the window to flutter at the curtains surrounding them. Francis had insisted on spending the night in the forest, where his supplies were, so he could be ready on the ground for his brother's arrival. Julian had, unsurprisingly, not bothered to convince him to stay.

"Why do you hate my uncle so?" Evie asked, when all they could hear was silence. Owls and songbirds alike were both resting; soon the sky would lighten and everything would change. The air would be full with the sounds of a midsummer morning.

And gunfire.

Julian sighed, rolling onto his front and propping himself up on his elbows before answering. "Because he followed us for so long. Because he thinks he knows me, but he doesn't. Because he thinks he knows *you* –"

"He is only trying to help," Evie said. She smiled softly. "Nobody knows me better than you, Julian. Certainly not as an adult. But my uncle isn't a bad man; far from it. He and your father were the only reason the country functioned for the first ten years of *my* father's rule."

Julian grumbled incoherently. He knew Evie was right, though he didn't want to admit it. He tucked a lock of Evie's hair behind her ear, allowing his fingertips to linger around it long enough to send a small wave of magic pulsing through her. The resultant flush of pleasure that crept up Evie's neck and cheeks had Julian kissing her before he could stop himself, though he knew that what the two of them had would eventually have to end.

He'd done something unforgivable to Evie, after all. Julian had imprisoned her for his own selfish reasons, never mind the fact that he'd also lied to her and made decisions on her behalf without considering what she thought of them. Julian didn't deserve her.

But he couldn't break away from Evie *now,* not with the king approaching and with her nestled into the crook of his arm, yawning herself to sleep. When the sun rose, and her father was dealt with, Julian would say his goodbyes.

"I love you," he murmured, just as Evie slipped into unconsciousness.

He wondered if she heard him.

CHAPTER TWENTY-SEVEN

Genevieve

When Evie awoke it was to the sound of cannon fire. She leapt out of bed; Julian was already awake, standing close enough to the window to see what was going on but not so close as to be seen himself.

She stalked over to his side. "Why didn't you wake me?"

Julian glanced at her for a moment before returning his gaze to the window. "I didn't want to disturb your sleep when all the king was doing was crossing the meadow. You should probably get dressed; he'll be at the foot of the tower soon."

Evie peered through the window somewhat nervously. "What was the cannon fire all about?"

"Intimidation, I guess," Julian chuckled, suggesting he wasn't scared in the slightest. "It makes no difference, anyway. Cannons run on gunpowder, and gunpowder is lit with fire."

Despite the dangerous situation they were in, there was something about the gleam in Julian's eyes that Evie loved. He was enthralling to watch when he was caught in the throes of the magic dwelling deep within him. Evie felt an inkling of what it must be like to be a human who possessed such power whenever he'd enchanted her hair. It was frightening and lovely in equal measure.

And he can wield it with minute control just as he can let it loose to devastating effect, she thought as she moved through to the bathroom to pull on a dress. It was a deep, sunset purple, transformed from a cloak Julian found in his father's stores. When he showed Evie the lower part of the tower she'd kicked a wall in frustration. To think that there had been so much more to the tower just below her feet – and for her not to have known of it – would eat away at her until the end of time.

Evie struggled to manoeuvre around her hair as she rejoined Julian. She wished she'd asked him to enchant it the night before; now it was too late. He needed every ounce of magic he could get, and her hair was the least of his problems.

"Wizard!" came the voice of her father hollering through the window, above the sounds of horses whinnying and men yelling to each other. "Show me that my daughter is unharmed or I will destroy your tower here and now!"

Julian smiled grimly, waving towards the window. "We'd be off to a bad start if he blasted us into the sky before I managed to work any magic," he joked. His hand lingered on Evie's when she walked past him; she squeezed it before reaching the window.

"I'll be fine," she murmured, then turned from Julian to address her father. He was resplendent in gold finery, sitting upon a large horse whose ebony hair shone in the sun. It pawed at the ground impatiently.

The king smiled up at her. "My lovely daughter. You are not hurt, I hope?"

Evie knew her father would try to sweet-talk her out of the tower the moment he opened his mouth. She supposed she couldn't blame him – she *had* been kidnapped, after all, and Evie had made no indication to him that she'd wanted to leave the palace.

"I am alive and well, father," she said. She gestured over the small battalion of cavalry her father had brought with him; in the rear were two deadly-looking cannons aimed directly at the tower. "Did you really need all this just to seek me out?"

He laughed bitterly. "You and I both know that Thorne's son is not to be taken lightly. Tell me, Genevieve, can you convince him to let you go? I will have mercy on him, for his father's sake, if he does."

"And what mercy is that?" Julian yelled, stepping forwards to stand beside Evie. The cannons swung to aim directly at him, though the king held up a hand to steady them.

"You will hit my daughter," he said. "Stand down." To Julian he called, "You brought your father's death upon you, boy. You defied your king, and now you have kidnapped a princess. The greatest mercy you can hope to receive now is a quick and painless death."

Evie knew her face had paled at the thought. All the blood in her seemed to rush out of her, leaving only cold. *It really will come down to my father's death or Julian's.*

Evie knew which of those options she couldn't bear to live with.

Down below it seemed as if the soldiers had grown uncomfortable, as had their horses. Their whinnying increased, and they hopped upon the grass as if it was burning them. When one of the soldiers cursed and threw his helmet to the floor Evie heard Julian cackle.

"Idiots," he muttered. "Did they really think I hadn't begun attacking already?"

Evie watched the king as he, in turn, watched his

240

soldiers with a frown. He hadn't been personally affected, but as the seconds stretched out it became apparent that Julian was slowly but surely cooking the men outside the tower.

"Don't kill them!" Evie told him, horrified.

He squeezed her hand in reassurance. "They'll have the worst sunburn of their life, and clothing will be unbearable to wear for a while, but they'll recover. The point is to drive them to distraction with the pain."

Evie supposed it was clever – the soldiers were certainly in disarray, no longer listening to their captain nor the king. The men controlling the cannons had to back away from them, for the metal sizzled and scorched their skin. On closer inspection Evie realised the cannons themselves were melting.

All the while Julian smiled pleasantly, as if slowly cooking a field of soldiers alive was no big deal whatsoever. But Evie could see his fingers beginning to twitch, and knew that even for him trying to control such a large quantity of magic must be tremendously difficult.

The king laughed up at him. "You think you can best me with that, Thorne? I thought you – ah!" He recoiled, almost thrown from his horse in the process, for Julian had shot out a barely-visible flare of magic which burst into flames inches from the king's face.

"I think you shouldn't underestimate me, *Your*

Majesty," Julian chided, though the trembling in his fingers was beginning to creep along his forearms. Evie resisted the urge to hold on to one of them to keep him stable; she didn't want her father to know how much Julian's wide-ranged attack was costing him.

How much energy is required to burn one hundred soldiers, their horses and two cannons? A lot, I imagine. For though Evie had witnessed Julian stun five men before, and set a table alight, and surround himself in fire, most of that magic had involved igniting a flame and setting it loose. Julian was a catalyst in those situations.

What he was doing now was much, much different.

"Y-your Majesty," one of the soldiers called out. Evie could scarcely look at him; his face had reddened and blistered and was beginning to weep. She felt sorry for him – she felt sorry for all of them – but she knew she couldn't stop Julian. Many of the soldiers had fainted from the pain his attack had inflicted, though a few still stood or knelt on the grass, moaning and screaming. Horses were bucking their riders off their backs, crying out in pain as they fled the meadow. She winced away at the sight before she knew what she was doing.

"See how my daughter turns away from what you're doing in horror, wizard!" the king cried, eyes shining triumphantly when he caught Evie's expression. "This is your last chance. Let her go."

Julian glanced at Evie; a bead of sweat rolled down

his forehead. "Ask her if she would like to go," he said, in lieu of a proper answer.

Her father cocked his head to one side. "Genevieve, of course you want to go. You're the heir to the throne. You're my daughter."

"You locked me up in here, father," she said, forcing herself to keep her voice hard and dispassionate.

"I did not know you were –"

"You told me some things were bigger than your love for me."

"Genevieve –"

"The pain you've caused to the people I love – to your entire country – is bigger than my love for *you*," Evie finished. She turned from the window so that she wouldn't have to see her father's face.

"You – you will come down here," her father spluttered, furious, "or I will force you to!"

"I can't hold this spell up for much longer," Julian admitted to her through gritted teeth. "I'm going to send out a final blast to knock them out, then – *get down*!"

Evie was thrown to the floor before she knew what had happened; Julian was hunched protectively over her. The bed was on fire. A few seconds later part of the wooden floor was, too, and then the door to the bathroom. Flaming arrows were streaming in through the

243

window, catching hold of anything that could be set alight.

"Time's up, wizard," she heard her father yell. "Send her down or you shall both perish!"

Julian stared at Evie with wide eyes. They reflected the flames consuming the room, though his irises were still full of magic. His skin was shining with sweat.

"Let go of your spell, Julian," Evie begged. "Let's get out of here. Let's –"

"Evie, your hair!"

Evie yelped when she spied a lick of flame crawling up the length of her hair, heading towards her at a sickening rate. She looked around frantically for water or a heavy blanket – anything to put it out. There was nothing.

But there *was* a knife.

"Evie, let me put it out for you," Julian heaved, barely conscious, but she pushed him aside, grabbed the blade and cut off her hair where it hit her shoulders. She barely made it in time; when the golden mass she'd cut off thumped to the floor it was engulfed in flame.

Evie grabbed Julian's trembling hand. "Drop the spell outside and get us out of here."

"I –"

"Do it!"

With a frown of concentration, and one final look at the flames consuming the tower all around them, Julian grabbed hold of Evie and snapped his fingers.

She hoped he'd stay conscious long enough to complete the spell.

CHAPTER TWENTY-EIGHT

Julian

All around was fire and chaos. Julian could smell the damage his and the king's flames had wrought upon the air – burning flesh, seared metal, a meadow turned to ash. He felt sick with it. Dimly he became away that he'd transported Evie and himself to the outskirts of the forest, where he knew Francis to be.

The trees are burning, he thought, looking up above him and seeing only fire. *So much destruction. Was that the king or was that me?* For the days had been long and dry for weeks now; the heat Julian had forced upon every living thing in front of the tower was more than capable of turning the entire area into a blaze.

"I should have simply killed the king," Julian coughed. His throat was raw and seared from smoke and flames and magic, and his eyes were stinging and blurred.

"You gave him a chance to stand down and he didn't take it," Evie insisted. Julian became aware that his arm was slung over her shoulders – Evie was supporting most of his weight as they walked as far from the burning tree line as possible. But there was nowhere they could go quickly enough to be of any use. Julian was exhausted. He knew he couldn't transport the two of them anywhere, and behind them he could hear the king on his horse, looking for them.

"You really thought that would work, wizard?" the king hollered. "Did you think I'd surrender because you burned my men? Even if you turned them to ash I wouldn't give up! Now hand me my daughter!"

Julian tripped on a fallen tree trunk and whined in pain – he didn't even have the strength to curse. Evie merely shifted more of his weight onto her.

"Come on, Julian," she panted. She was covered in sweat and soot and ash, her newly-shortened hair dull and uneven from the filthy blade she'd used to cut it. "We can do it. Just a little further. We just have to find my uncle. We just have to –"

"No," Julian sighed, and he dropped to the forest

247

floor. "No, I can't go any further, Evie. I don't have the strength."

There were furious tears in Evie's eyes as she tried to force him back up. "Come on, you idiot! Don't give up now! What was the point of taking a stand against the king if you don't survive it? Get up!"

Julian merely shook his head. With aching, trembling fingers he ran a hand through Evie's hair. He laughed noiselessly when he reached the end of it so quickly. "You cut your hair."

"Yes; it was either that or burn alive."

"The former sounds like a much better idea."

Evie let out a garbled sob at the ridiculous joke. "My hair will grow back. The rest of me would not." She ran the back of her hand across Julian's brow, and although he knew her skin must have been burning hot it felt cool against the inferno raging inside of him.

"Evie, you have to let me send you somewhere safe," Julian insisted, as loudly as he could. "I don't know where Francis is, and your father is almost upon us. Let me –"

"I am *not* leaving you behind," Evie cried. "If he finds us, he finds us, but I won't let him touch you! He'll have to kill me first!"

"Evie, he'll use you as a puppet to the people and

keep you prisoner to his will if he thinks he has leverage against you," Julian reminded her. He coughed and hacked on the smoke rapidly filling the forest. Neither of them could see much further past the other one's face. "He already has your mother and brother. Don't allow him to use me against you, too. Let me send you away."

"Julian –"

The air was split by the cracking of a bullet. Julian stilled, and Evie too. It was close by. When they heard another Evie dug her nails into Julian's arm; it kept him clinging to consciousness even though his mind so eagerly wanted to slip away.

"Who goes there?" the king demanded. Through the sounds of burning and screaming Julian could just barely make out the sound of the man's horse upon the forest floor, several feet to his left.

"A stranger," Francis growled, and then the king's horse screamed in fright; Julian heard it topple to the ground, so close he could smell its singed mane.

"You bastard!" Pierre exclaimed between grunts and shouts. Clearly the two of them were fighting, though neither Julian nor Evie could see what was going on.

She squeezed his hand. "How much magic would it take to clear the air?" she asked, very quietly.

"I would not want to risk Francis' advantage."

"We will choke to death on this smoke before long."

"Then let me -"

"*Don't* say you want to send me away. I'm staying with you, Julian."

He sighed, before sending just enough magic out into the air to clear the smoke in the immediate vicinity. The relief on his and Evie's lungs was immediate; Julian's head felt altogether clearer the moment he took a clean breath.

Evie's eyes darted to her father's horse. The beast hadn't been hurt from what Julian could see, though it was struggling to get back to its feet. Evie crawled over to it, whispering reassurances as she urged it upright.

"Do you think you can get on him?" she asked Julian.

"If I said no, what would you do?"

"Force you onto him somehow."

"You're a weak, skinny brat."

"So it will make *you* look even more pathetic when I manage it."

Julian chuckled despite himself and then, with a tremendous amount of effort, hauled himself to his feet. Evie brought the horse over to him, allowing him to use her arm in order to help him up onto the animal. Then she jumped up in front of him, took hold of the reins and urged the horse forwards.

"Let's get out of here before my father finds –"

Just as Evie spoke both the king and his brother appeared in front of them. They were smeared with blood and grime and ash; for a moment Julian could not tell which was which. But then the king turned his head to stare at them, furious.

"You would dare attempt to escape on *my* horse!" he raged, but then Francis slashed a knife across his cheek and he focused back on their fight.

"Get out of here!" Francis urged. He dodged out of the way when Pierre sent a punch his way, then fired back with one of his own.

Evie and Julian didn't have to be told twice. They wound their way through the burning trees, the horse beneath them following its own instincts to escape the fire more than paying attention to where Evie directed him. Julian took a deep breath, fought back the urge to throw up, then sent out several tendrils of magic to find the stream than ran through the forest.

"What are you doing, Julian?!" Evie screamed back at him when she felt his head droop down to her shoulder. "Stop using magic!"

"Just a little bit," he mumbled, closing his eyes in order to focus on dowsing the fire around them. He sent water to the meadow, too, to sooth the agonised soldiers, and then when he was sure the blaze itself was extinguished he added a little healing magic to the water to relieve them of their wounds.

"Julian, that's enough," Evie said, her voice trembling. "Whatever you're doing, it's enough. You're going to kill yourself."

By the time they made their way back to the meadow most of the soldiers were lying on the burned grass. Their horses were huddled some distance away from the dirty steam filling the air around their riders. Nobody had died.

Good, Julian thought dully. *Good. No deaths.*

"Princess," the captain said when he spied the pair of them. He frowned at the king's horse. "What is going on? What is –"

"My brother is dead."

They all turned; Francis appeared from the forest, limping heavily. He dragged the king's body behind him, though he dropped him as soon as he reached the meadow.

"General Francis!" the captain exclaimed, alarmed, and he drew his sword. "You have killed the –"

"Stand down," Evie ordered. She sat up straighter on her father's horse, though she kept her hands on Julian's arms wound around her waist to keep him upright behind her. He was grateful, for without her support he'd have likely fallen.

The captain faltered.

"Stand down," she repeated. "You heard yourself that my father named me heir to the throne, did you not? And even if you argue that the title remains my brother's, I am still your princess, and I am telling you to stand down. Do you defy me?"

"I wouldn't dare to," Julian muttered into her ear. He felt Evie's lips quirk into a smile more than he saw it, for in a moment it was gone.

"My father was not a good man," she called out to the soldiers. "He painted my uncle as a war criminal and exiled him for a personal slight. He imprisoned The Thorn Wizard and murdered him in cold blood to enrage his son. The queen and my little brother are also held prisoner in the palace. Do you truly wish to follow my father's orders, or will you instead follow mine?"

The captain surveyed his soldiers, who were watching both Evie and Julian in awed terror. He inclined his head. "And what are your orders, Princess Genevieve?"

She squeezed Julian's arm. "Take us to the nearest inn where we all can recover, then escort us back to Willow."

It was then, and only then, that Julian passed out, and

did not wake for a long, long time.

CHAPTER TWENTY-NINE

Genevieve

"How long do you think he'll sleep for, mama?"

"For as long as he needs, I imagine."

"If Julian had his way then that would mean three months," Evie muttered. Julian was so still upon the bed he lay in that a stranger might have believed he was no longer alive. "He's been asleep for ten days, mama. By anyone's measure that's a long, long time."

Queen Mariette smiled softly at her daughter. "Perhaps he needs to heal more than just his injuries, my love. He's been through a lot."

Evie, Francis and Julian had arrived at the palace the day before. They'd headed back on horses as quickly as they were able to after the debacle at the tower, though word had been sent ahead to the queen of what had transpired. Knowing that her husband was dead, and that herself, her children and Francis were free seemed to have added years to the woman's life; already she looked much better than she had done when Evie was first reunited with her.

But Evie had a burning question for her mother that would no doubt bring up bad memories. She didn't want to burden her after everything she'd been through, but Evie *needed* answers. She couldn't rest until she did.

"...mama," she said, before leaving Julian's bedside to stand in front of a mirror. Evie had washed and washed her hair until no trace of fire and destruction lay within it, and her mother had brought someone in to cut the ends evenly so that it sat nicely around her shoulders, but the lack of weight on her head unsettled her deeply. Evie felt like she'd lost a limb – some integral part of her very being that made her who she was.

"What is it, Evie?" her mother asked, following her to the mirror with a brush in hand. They sat in front of it, and Evie allowed her to brush through her hair as she had done when she was a child. But it wasn't enough.

It was Julian's hands she wanted to feel on her scalp, weaving golden crowns into her hair.

"Why did you lie about who my father was?" Evie asked. She fidgeted with her fingers in her lap. Was she ready for the answer to her question?

"I didn't – I never knew if you were Pierre or Francis' child," her mother replied. She sighed heavily. "I could have asked Jacques to check for me when you were born, but that would have raised suspicion. He didn't find out about me and Francis until you were around six, you see, and by then it seemed inconsequential whose chose child you really were."

"But then why did you say that uncle was my father, when you were found out?"

"Because I knew Pierre would send you away if you were. I hoped you would escape; I was so happy when I discovered you *had*. I wanted you to live a normal life free from the reach of your father. Had he known you were his daughter he'd never have let you go, and he would stop me from seeing you in order to punish me."

Evie stayed silent as she digested all of this information. Her mother's plan had been flawed, for sure, but Evie saw the sense in it. Twelve years locked in a tower was far better than a lifetime of indentured servitude to her father, especially if she had been raised not to know what it was that he was doing.

"The last time your hair was this length, you were five," her mother said, working out a tug as gently as possible as she spoke. "Louis' hair got as long as yours

257

did when he reached that age, but Pierre made me cut it. Your brother cried for days about it."

Evie laughed softly. "I'd have loved to see it. How is he?"

Her mother didn't respond, instead gesturing in the mirror towards the half-open door. Evie could just barely see the boy in question standing there, watching them.

"Louis, don't you want to come in?" Evie asked, turning from the mirror to smile at him directly. He returned it with an anxious one of his own as he padded across the carpet to join them.

"I can? I really can?"

"But of course! Why would you think I'd say no?"

He looked at the floor. "Papa always –"

"Papa isn't here to tell you no," Evie said firmly, "but I'm here to tell you yes."

Louis perked up upon hearing his sister's answer, though that wasn't saying much. In contrast to his mother, he looked even sicker than the last time Evie had seen him.

So frail and small, she thought. *And no amount of eating like a piglet can save him.* Reaching out her arms for Louis, the boy gladly climbed onto her lap and lay against her chest. Evie rested her chin on his head, which caused Louis to giggle.

"Your hair tickles," he said, wrinkling his nose when several strands of it swept across his face. "I thought you said you wouldn't cut it yet?"

"I said I'd cut it *some day.* I guess that day came."

"I'd say cutting it under threat of fiery oblivion doesn't count as you doing it willingly."

Evie froze. She stared at the mirror, past herself and her little brother, only to realise that her mother was no longer sitting right behind them. She was standing over by the bedside, giving a very grumpy, very groggy wizard a glass of water.

"Julian!" Evie cried. She carried Louis straight over with her to Julian's bedside, excited as she was. "I can't believe you're awake! You've been asleep for ten days. *Ten days.* Can you believe –"

"Will you shut up?" Julian muttered. Both the queen and Louis looked horrified that he would say such a thing to Evie, but when they saw her smile they relaxed. He glanced at her brother. "So this is Louis. Huh. He looks just like you."

"Because I'm a brat," Evie said. "I get it."

Julian quirked an eyebrow. "I was going to say you share the same hair and eyes, but that'll do." He held out his hand to the boy. "How do you do, Your Majesty? He *is* the king now, isn't he? Or did you – Evie, you didn't actually take up the throne, did you?"

"No need to sound so terrified of such a prospect," she laughed. "But no. I'm not...I'm not ready to be the queen of anything. I have so much to learn. My uncle will act as regent until Louis comes of age, or..."

Evie didn't finish her sentence. They all knew what she meant, even Louis himself.

Julian stretched his arms over his head and cracked his neck to one side. "That reminds me. Queen Mariette, what is it exactly that ails your son?"

"A disease of the blood," she said sadly, drooping her head as she did so. "It's afflicted Louis for years. Nobody can find a cure."

"I can see one with my own eyes."

Evie frowned. "What are you talking about – ah!"

Julian had snatched her hand and pricked the meat of her thumb open with a pin; she didn't even know where he got it from. *It was probably stashed up his sleeve,* she thought. *He always kept god knows what inside that old cloak of his, after all.*

"May I have your hand, Your Majesty?" he asked Louis, though the boy seemed a little frightened after watching what had happened to his sister.

"It doesn't hurt, Louis, I swear," Evie reassured him. "Julian just surprised me."

"Okay..." the boy said, still uncertain as he gave his

tiny hand over to Julian. The wizard grinned at him and, before Louis had a chance to realise what had happened, Julian pricked his thumb.

"Well isn't this a lucky turn of events," he muttered, rubbing the two drops of blood he'd obtained from the siblings between his fingers.

"It's a match?!" the queen exclaimed. "Is it a – it's a match?"

Julian nodded. "Completely. It will take a while, but regular transfusions from Evie to her brother will clean up his blood and cure his disease. I'd say once every three weeks for four months, then every two months thereafter for a year or so. Evie will need to get plenty of bed rest and lots of food to regain her blood quickly... which shouldn't be a problem." He gave her a wry smile, but Evie was too emotional to return it. She knew she was crying but she didn't care.

She looked from Julian to her mother to Louis then back again. "And that will fix him? That will actually cure him?"

"Would I be telling you to do this if it wouldn't?"

"I – no. Thank you, Julian. Thank you!"

Evie would have thrown her arms around him, had her mother not done so first. Her body was wracked with silent sobs. Evie instead wrapped her arms around her brother, who looked up at her with disbelieving eyes.

261

"I'm going to be okay?"

"Just so long as you keep me company when I'm growing more blood, then yes!"

He giggled when Evie planted a kiss on his forehead. "Do you think we'll look even more alike if I have your blood in me?"

"Who knows? I guess we'll have to find out."

The room was full of excited chatter and thanks for Julian for another few minutes, then the queen lifted Louis into her arms and made for the door. "I shall give the two of you some privacy," she said, smiling. "I will arrange for a doctor to arrive first thing in the morning if that suits you, Evie."

She nodded, and then her mother was gone.

Julian did not say anything for a while. Evie couldn't bring herself to break the silence, either, though before she knew it her hand had found itself intertwined with Julian's.

Eventually he drew in a deep breath. "Evie –"

"I know."

He frowned. "You –"

"You have to leave. I know, so don't say it." She stared at him miserably. "I don't blame you for what you did. You were in pain. You didn't mean to do it."

"Yet I did it all the same." Julian squeezed her hand. "I need to be by myself for a while, Evie, to clear my head. To work through my grief and anger. What happened to me...I cannot afford for that to happen again. I don't want to ever hurt you."

"But it isn't fair!" Evie cried. "Julian, I love –"

"No," he interrupted. Though he was smiling, Julian's eyes were too tight, and his grip on Evie's hand reflected that. "Don't say it. Not now."

She pushed against his chest. "You got to say it when you thought I was sleeping."

He chuckled. "Then I suppose I really *am* being unfair. Goodbye, Princess Genevieve."

And then Julian clicked his fingers, and he was gone.

"Not now, he said," Evie mumbled as she forced herself to dry her tears and get to her feet. She had to keep all her strength for Louis; now was not the time for crying. "I won't tell you *now,* then, Julian."

Evie could wait. After all, she'd spent twelve years of her life waiting in his tower to meet him.

EPILOGUE

Julian

Julian was nursing a tankard of ale in the corner of a tavern, hating himself.

Fourteen months had passed since Francis Saule had become regent. Louis had made a remarkable recovery from his illness, thanks to Evie's blood, and with her imprisonment finally over Mariette's health was much improved, too. Between them all they were working to fix everything King Pierre had destroyed, ignored or otherwise made a mess of. Julian had heard in several towns and villages that the queen was restarting her tours of the country, too. People were excited to have her back.

And where am I over a year later? Julian wondered. *Drinking in the inn where Evie and I first stayed the night after I saved her life. She drank a cup of wine believing it to be water.* He snorted in amusement, drawing the gazes of several curious bar-goers in the process.

Despite his promise to himself that he would not let his hair grow as long as it had been before, Julian had failed miserably at keeping said promise. It was currently tied back to keep it away from his face. It properly fell to his shoulders now – the length Evie's hair had been when she cut it free from the flames rapidly engulfing it.

I wonder if I should let it grow longer and longer, just to annoy her, Julian thought, amused by such a notion. *At least I've been shaving my face. Well...most of the time.* He ran a hand over his jaw, where several days' worth of stubble grew. He grimaced. *I'm certainly better dressed than I was when I first met Evie.*

Julian hated that he had to think of such trivial improvements to mark that he'd done anything of worth in the last fourteen months. Evie was in Willow, learning how to rule a country alongside her brother – a brother she was directly responsible for saving the life of. She was flourishing. The people adored her. For how could they not?

She could not have done all of that if I was with her,

Julian knew, for he would never have wished to stay in Willow long enough for Evie to enact any kind of positive change. And he couldn't bear the thought of staying in the palace, where his father had died. The expansive, beautiful building felt like far worse a prison to Julian than his father's tower ever had.

Though Evie might object to me saying as much. The tower was burned to rubble, anyway, though Jacques Thorne's stores of elixirs, spell books, curses and clothing had remained untouched. Julian had since paid for a house to be rebuilt there, using stones from the original tower wherever possible. Many of them had been scorched beyond repair in the fire, but there had been enough to build one of the walls and a chimney of the new house. Julian hadn't moved into it yet, though it had been completed weeks ago.

He wasn't sure he ever could.

"Mister Thorne, there's a visitor for you up in your room."

Julian stilled, fingers tensing on his tankard just a little too much. He hadn't told the innkeeper his name.

"Ah, Mister Thorne," the man repeated, nervously this time. "Forgive me, but the lady really was insistent about letting you know she was here. She told me I should call you Mister Thorne. My apologies."

Julian frowned. "The lady?"

He nodded. "Beautiful woman. Gold hair like you rarely see in these parts. Something really special –"

Julian was out of his seat and flying up the stairs before the innkeeper could finish his sentence. *Don't be ridiculous,* he thought, barely daring to believe what – or who – might be waiting for him inside his room. *I told her to stay away. I told her.*

"Evie," he breathed, the moment he slammed open the door. Her hair was woven down her back; it reached below her shoulder blades now.

She smiled when she saw the look on his face, and took a few steps towards him. "*Not now,* you said a year ago. Not now. Have I waited enough time?"

"What are you talking about?" Julian asked, dizzy from his sprint up the stairs and the sight of the woman before him. "What are you –"

"I love you, Julian," Evie said, closing the distance between them just as he reached out for her. "Am I allowed to say that now?"

"You're – you were in Willow."

"I'm taking over my mother's tours of the country," Evie explained. She crawled her hands up Julian's chest as if she barely believed him to be real. "But not for another year or two."

"So what are you doing so far away from the city?"

267

She slid her hands down until they found Julian's. He held them tightly, though he hated that he was shaking. Evie looked down at them, interlacing her fingers through Julian's and squeezing his hands until the shaking stopped.

"I thought I might...see some of the world first. You know, to combat my wilful ignorance. Do you know of anyone who might act as my willing guide? I hear there's a faerie trapped as a fox that I'd quite like to see with my own eyes."

Julian bent his head down until his nose touched Evie's. "You are...so annoying. This trip sounds so annoying. One or two years of you never shutting up, and eating all of my money, and complaining about being *cold*, and –"

"Is that a yes?"

"I guess it must be," he said, and he kissed her. Evie let go of his hands to guide her own through his hair, untying it in the process. When she saw it fell to Julian's shoulders she gasped.

"Your hair is so long! Why haven't you cut it?"

His lips quirked into a smile. "I'll cut it if you cut yours."

EXTRA CHAPTER

Genevieve

"Remind me *never* to travel by boat again, Julian."

Evie's face was pale and sallow. She stood hunched over the wooden railing of the ship they'd boarded to get them across the channel, having spent the last half an hour heaving into the sea. There was nothing left in her stomach anymore.

"You're the one who wanted to see the fair folk," Julian pointed out, rubbing Evie's back before he eased her over to a wooden bench bolted onto the deck.

She made a face. "I thought you might have, oh, I

don't know, *clicked your fingers* and we'd be there already."

"Using transportation magic across a single country is one thing – over multiple lands is another entirely."

"Does it take too much energy?" Evie asked, releasing all the air from her lungs as she leaned against the bench. Julian smoothed her hair away from her face – the ends of it reached the small of her back now.

"Yes and no," Julian replied, frowning at the horizon. "It does take more energy, but not so much that I couldn't do it. The problem is that I don't know the British Isles the way I do our home. If I don't know exactly where I'm transporting to – a pinpoint location – then the magic is likely to go...awry. I think you'd like that far less than being sick over the deck of a ship."

"Please don't talk about being sick." Julian smirked in response; Evie didn't like the mischievous look on his face at all. "What?" she demanded, crossing her arms over her chest until she realised that it made her feel worse. Evie bowed her head instead, breathing shallow and laboured as she fought the urge to retch.

The wizard laughed. "I can stop you feeling nauseous, you know. I must admit I'm beginning to feel genuinely sorry for you."

Evie froze for a moment. She looked up at Julian very, very slowly. "You could have stopped me feeling like this and you're only mentioning it *now*?"

He shrugged. "You're the one who wanted to experience the world. I figured that meant even the bad stuff."

"I'd have been more than happy to skip over sea sickness!"

"You might not have been affected by it, though," Julian reasoned. "There's no point wasting magic until I know it's needed."

Evie glared at him. "It. *Is.* Needed."

Julian laughed once more, then splayed his fingertips across her forehead. "You might have been alright had you not pigged out at lunch," he murmured, but upon seeing Evie grit her teeth he grew silent.

A few seconds later and Julian's magic had snaked its way through Evie's entire body, easing her nausea, relaxing the spasms in her stomach and eliminating the pain in her skull. She became aware that he had also woven magic into her hair, though it wasn't long enough to warrant needing it for practicality's sake.

Show off, was all Evie thought as she felt the braids Julian enchanted her hair into forming. When he removed his fingers Evie closed her eyes and breathed deeply.

When she opened them she felt completely fine, all

traces of her previous sickness gone.

"Thank you," she muttered, "though I'd say this was all your fault in the first place, Julian."

He rolled his eyes before planting a kiss on her forehead. "At least now you know what sea sickness feels like, so you need never experience it again."

"Wonderful. I think I need something to eat." The subsequent rumble from Evie's stomach backed up her claim.

Julian smiled as he stood up and stretched. "I guess we better head below deck, then."

The two of them crossed the deck towards the stairs, Evie stumbling a little on her feet as she fought to regain her balance, when she became aware of an oddly familiar couple standing by the bow of the ship.

She frowned. "Julian, aren't they the ones who were watching us in that town, back when you were taking me to Willow?"

"We are indeed!" called the woman by the bow, which caught both Evie and Julian by surprise. She turned her head, lustrous hair shining in the sunlight, and smiled at them. "My name's Scarlett Duke. Won't you join us for a while?"

Evie raised an uncertain eyebrow at Julian. "Should we...?"

"You were the one who wanted to eat."

"I think I can hold off for a few minutes for curiosity's sake."

Julian made a non-committal noise in the back of his throat, slipped an arm around Evie's waist to stop her from stumbling against the rolling waves beneath them, then led her over to where Scarlett and her mysterious companion were waiting.

This close up Evie could see that the woman was even more beautiful than she'd thought the first time she'd seen her. Scarlett's blue eyes were rich and dark against her pale skin, and her hair was wound over one shoulder in a thick, heavy braid all the way to her waist.

It won't be long until my hair is longer than that again, Evie thought as she fingered the ends of her own hair.

Scarlett's lips quirked in amusement. "Your hair is certainly much shorter than it was last time I saw you, Princess Genevieve."

Evie took half a step away from her, discomfited. "How do you know who I am?"

Scarlett inclined her head towards the man standing beside her, who was looking out towards the horizon. "Adrian worked it out. Well, he used magic to work it out, which isn't the same as using your brain, so –"

273

"Charming," the man named Adrian interrupted, casting a sidelong glance at Evie in the process. His amber eyes were alarming to behold at such close-range; Julian's arm tightened around Evie.

"You're a magician," Julian said, narrowing his eyes at Adrian. "I should have known."

"And you're a wizard, going by the princess' hair," Adrian replied. "Impressive work, though I'm loathe to admit it."

Scarlett clucked her tongue. "That wasn't very nice, Adrian."

"Wizards are always full of themselves," he countered, as if a very powerful wizard who could most certainly burn him to ashes if he was offended by such a comment wasn't standing right in front of him. "They're born with the smallest affinity for magic and they think they're so much better than –"

"Most of us *are* better at our craft than you, magician," Julian said. "That's the point of being born into it. Talent for a subject very rarely trumps a natural-born magic-user."

Evie pulled away from Julian, confused. "Didn't you once tell me that the line between the two was getting blurred, and soon there would be no need for two separate terms...?"

Adrian laughed even as Julian ran an exasperated

hand over his face. "Is that so, wizard?" he asked. "Are we not so dissimilar, after all?"

Julian glared at him. "I'd like to see *you* weave an enchantment like the one in Evie's hair."

"Oh, I'd never be able to do it," Adrian replied without a shred of disappointment. "My expertise lies in curses."

"Of course it does."

"And what is that supposed to mean?"

"It means," Scarlett interrupted, holding an arm out in front of Adrian to push him back just as Evie did the same to Julian, "that the two of you are very clearly talented men, and there's no use getting into a fight to see who's better with magic than the other."

"Especially not when I know at least one of you could set the entire ship on fire," Evie muttered, digging her fingernails into Julian's arm when he still didn't back down. His eyes were beginning to glow. "I'd rather that didn't happen."

Julian glanced at her, then at Scarlett and Adrian, then back to Evie. He took a few steps back and shook his head. "You're right. Miss Duke, my apologies. I didn't mean to lose my temper."

Evie frowned. "Do *I* not get an apology?"

Julian bent down until his lips were by her ear. "I'll

apologise to you later," he murmured, in a tone that suggested very few words were likely to be spoken during said apology. Evie's cheeks flushed slightly at the insinuation.

Adrian bowed his head politely. "I'm sorry, Princess Genevieve. It's very unbecoming of me to act in such a manner. I should know better."

Scarlett chuckled. "Yes, you should. I haven't seen you this competitive since Sam asked me to marry him."

"That was justified!"

"Is that so?"

Evie stared at the two of them in wonder. "The two of you are...interesting," she blurted out loud, without thinking about how the statement actually sounded.

Adrian raised an eyebrow; a scar ran through it, splitting it in two. "Is that an insult, or a compliment?"

"Compliment, of course!" Evie insisted, though out of the corner of her eye she saw Julian mouth the word *insult* very clearly. She elbowed him in the ribs before returning her attention to Scarlett and Adrian. "Where are you from?"

"Germany," Scarlett said. "We're your next door neighbours, as it were."

"I've never been there before," Evie admitted, "though you have, haven't you, Julian?"

276

"Once. It's pretty enough, I suppose."

Evie had to fight the urge to shout at him. She'd never seen Julian so disgruntled by a human being that wasn't her uncle before.

Scarlett ignored the back-handed compliment. "Where are the two of you headed now? We're visiting London for the time being."

"Scotland," Julian answered. The hint of a smile played across his lips – he was looking forward to reaching the country just as much as Evie herself was. "We're on the hunt for a fox."

"I take it this is no ordinary fox," Adrian murmured, cocking his head to one side in interest. "I've avoided the fair folk myself, given their propensity to turn people into animals."

Scarlett laughed before kissing him on the cheek. "You have so much experience in that area, though. You'd probably thrive in Scotland."

"Perhaps...if wolves hadn't become extinct there last century."

When Evie's stomach rumbled insistently everyone looked at her. She flushed with embarrassment. "Sorry," she mumbled, staring at the floor, "I might be a little hungry."

"Well how about we all head below deck for

something to eat?" Scarlett suggested, much to the horror of both Adrian and Julian. She moved forward and linked an arm with Evie. "Or the two of us could go and leave these sorry men to fend for themselves. I'm fascinated to know your story, Princess Genevieve."

"Call me Evie," she replied, giggling when she realised the men in question were watching them walk away with shocked expressions upon both their faces. "Though I must admit I think Adrian and your story seems far more interesting than my own."

"I suppose it might be, but it's a story I know, whereas I don't know yours."

"I guess that means both our stories may be just as interesting as the other."

Scarlett beamed. "Exactly."

They barely made it to the stairs before Julian and Adrian caught up with them. "Don't you dare leave me with him, Evie," Julian muttered under his breath when he reached her side. "Otherwise I might burn his other eyebrow clean off."

"I heard that, wizard," Adrian said.

"Good."

"*Julian!*"

Evie and Scarlett both let out equally resigned sighs, then laughed at each other. It was clear from Julian's face that he didn't understand how the two of them could have become friends quite as quickly as they had done.

"I think the rest of the journey should pass rather pleasantly," Scarlett said as they all sat down at a large table. Julian sat as far from Adrian as was physically possible, much to Evie's amusement. Scarlett wound her arm through Adrian's just as he nuzzled his nose against her face.

"Yes, so very pleasant," Adrian said, firing a glare at Julian before returning his attention to Scarlett.

Evie interlaced her hand with Julian's below the table, then leant her head against his shoulder. "Consider this part of your apology," she murmured, "though I still expect one in private."

Julian kissed her hair and smiled softly.

"I guess, if it's for you, I can deal with that."

PRINCE OF FOXES CHAPTER ONE

Lachlan

Today was the queen's funeral and Lachlan, her only child and heir to the throne, was deliberately avoiding the ceremony.

His mother would understand, he was sure. He'd never been one for mournful occasions; most of the Seelie folk weren't. Their lives were long enough to be considered immortal by the humans who largely lived, unknowing and unseeing, beside them. If Lachlan allowed himself to be truly sad he'd spend centuries feeling that way.

It was the last thing he wanted.

So Lachlan was currently whiling away his morning following a human girl who was collecting early autumn brambles on the outskirts of the forest. She lived in Darach, the closest human settlement to the central realm of the Scots fair folk. The people who lived there were, in general, respectful and wary of Lachlan and his kind. They saw what members of the Seelie Court could do fairly regularly, after all. The rest of the British Isles was another story entirely, though it hadn't always been that way.

Everybody in the forest knew things were changing.

The advancements made in human medicine, and human technology, and human ingenuity, meant that humans were beginning to forget what it felt like to fear 'otherness'. They believed themselves above tales of faeries, and magic in general, though Lachlan knew there were humans capable of magic, too.

Not here, though, he thought, creeping from one tall bow of an oak tree to another to trail silently after the girl. She was happily eating one bramble for every two she placed in her basket, seemingly without a care in the world. *Not on this island. Not for centuries.* Lachlan knew this was largely because his mother, Queen Evanna

– as well as King Eirian of the Unseelie Court far down south, in England – spirited all such magically-inclined British children away to the faerie realm, to live for all intents and purposes as faeries themselves.

That's certainly better than being an ordinary human, especially now, when they've forgotten about us.

A stiff breeze tearing through the oak tree caused Lachlan's solitary earring to jingle like a bell. Adorned with delicate chains and tiny sapphires, and spanning the entire length of his long, pointed ear as a cuff of beaten silver, the beautiful piece of jewellery had been a gift from his mother from a time long since passed. Back then Lachlan had been enamoured with the blue-eyed faerie, Ailith, and had been convinced the two of them would marry. The earring was ultimately meant as a gift for Ailith, he'd decided. His mother would never be so direct as to give it to Lachlan's beloved herself. It wasn't in her nature.

But then Queen Evanna had married the half-Unseelie faerie, Innis, who was the Unseelie king's brother. He had himself a grown son, Fergus, who came with his father to live in the Seelie realm. The two were silver where Lachlan and his mother were gold, and Ailith had become betrothed to his new-found stepbrother instead of him.

So Lachlan lost his love and, now, he'd lost his mother. The earring was all he had left of both.

I should go to the funeral, he decided, turning from the girl as he did so. *I am to be king, after all. I should –*

Lachlan paused. He could hear something. More chime-like than his earring in the wind, and clearer than the sound of the nearby stream flowing over centuries-smooth stone.

The human girl was singing.

"The winds were laid, the air was still,

The stars they shot alang the sky;

The fox was howling on the hill,

And the distant echoing glens reply."

Lachlan was enamoured with the sound of her voice. The words were Burns; the melody unfamiliar. He thought perhaps she'd invented the tune herself and, if so, she was a talented girl indeed. He peered through the yellowing leaves of the oak tree, intent on seeing what the human with the lovely voice truly looked like.

She was not so much a girl as a young woman – perhaps not quite twenty – though since Lachlan himself had lived for almost five times that long she was, for all intents and purposes, still simply a girl. Her skin was pale and lightly freckled, though her cheeks held onto some colour from the fast-fading summer. Her hair was a little darker than the oak trunk Lachlan was currently leaning against. It flashed like deep copper when it caught the sunlight and hung long and wild down her back, which was a sight rarely seen on a young, human woman.

A cream dress fell to her ankles and sat low on her shoulders. Small leather boots, made for wandering through forests and across meadows, were laced across her feet. A cloak of pine-coloured fabric was slung over the handle of her almost-full wicker basket. *Well-made clothes,* he concluded, *but nothing elaborate or expensive. Just an ordinary girl.* She dithered over the correct words of the next verse of her Burns poem as Lachlan merrily watched on. *Fair to look at, for a human. But it is her voice that is special. Special enough to ask her name.*

He delighted over thinking how his stepfather and stepbrother would react when he brought back a human girl, enchanted to sing for him until the end of time. *I wonder what Ailith would think. Would she be jealous? Would she mourn for the loss of my attention?*

Lachlan was excited to find out.

He stretched his arms above his head, causing his earring to jingle once more. Below him the girl stilled. She stopped singing, dark brows knitted together in confusion.

"Is somebody there?" she asked, carefully placing her basket down by her feet as she spoke.

"You have a lovely voice," Lachlan announced. He

was satisfied to see the girl jump in fright, eyes swinging wildly around before she realised the voice she'd heard came from above. When she spied Lachlan standing high up on the boughs of the oak tree she gasped.

"You are – it is early to see one of your kind so far out of the forest," she said. She struggled to maintain a blank face, to appear as if she wasn't surprised in the slightest to see a faerie standing in a tree.

Lachlan laughed. "I suppose it is. Today is a special occasion; we are all very much wide awake."

The girl seemed to hesitate before responding. Lachlan figured she was trying to decide if it was wise to continue such a conversation with him. "What occasion would be so special to have you all awake before noon?"

"The funeral of the queen. My mother."

"Oh."

That was all she said. Lachan had to wonder what kind of reaction he'd expected. Certainly not sympathy; he had no use for such a thing.

"You are not at the funeral?" the girl asked after a moment of silence. "If you are her son –"

"I shall get there eventually," Lachlan replied. He sat down upon the branch he'd been standing on. "Tell me your name, lass. Your voice is too beautiful to not have a name attached to it."

To his surprise, she smiled. "I do not think so, Prince of Faeries."

Clever girl.

"You wound me," he said, holding a hand over his heart in mock dismay. "An admirer asks only for a name and you will not oblige his lowly request? How cruel you are."

"How about a name for a name, then?" she suggested. "That seems fair."

Lachlan nodded in agreement. The girl could do nothing with his name. She was only human.

"Lachlan," he replied, with a flourish of his hand in place of a bow. "And you?"

"Clara."

"A pretty name for a pretty girl. Is there a family name to go with –"

"I am not so much a fool as to give you my family name," Clara said, "and I think you know that."

He found himself grinning. "Maybe so. Come closer, Clara. You stand so far away."

He was somewhat surprised when she boldly took a step forwards, half expecting her to decide enough was enough and run away. *Even careful humans give in to the allure of faeries,* he thought, altogether rather smug. *It won't be long until I have Clara's full name.*

When Clara took another step towards him Lachlan noticed that her eyes were green.

No, blue, he decided. *No, they're –*

"Your eyes," he said, deftly swinging backwards until he was hanging upside down from the branch. Lachlan's face was now level with Clara's, though the wrong way round. She took a shocked half-step backwards at their new-found proximity. "They are strange."

"I do not think my eyes are as strange as yours, Lachlan of the forest," she replied. "Yours are gold."

"Not so uncommon a colour for a Seelie around these parts. Yours, on the other hand...we do not see mismatched eyes often."

Clara shrugged. "One blue, one green. They are not so odd. Most folk hardly notice a difference unless they stand close to me."

"Do many human boys get as close to you as I am now?" Lachlan asked, a smile playing across his lips at the blush that crossed Clara's cheeks.

She looked away. "I cannot say they have."

"Finish your song for me, Clara. I'll give you something in return."

"And what would that be?" she asked, glancing back

at Lachlan. Her suspicion over the sudden change of subject was written plainly on her face.

He swung himself forwards just a little until their lips were almost touching. "A kiss, of course."

"That's...and what if I do not want that?"

"Then I guess I leave with a broken heart."

Clara's eyebrow quirked.

"You do not believe me," he complained.

"With good reason."

"You really are a cruel girl."

The two stared at each other for a while, though Lachlan was beginning to grow dizzy from his upside down view. But just as he was about to right himself, Clara took a deep breath and began to sing once more.

There were four verses left of her Burns poem, about a ghost who appeared in front of the poet to lament over what happened to him in the final years of his life, and it was both haunting and splendid to hear. Lachlan mourned for the spirit as if it had been real, and wished there was more to the poem for Clara to sing.

But eventually she sang her last, keening note, leaving only the sound of the wind to break their silence. When Lachlan crept a hand behind her neck and urged her lips to his Clara fluttered her eyes closed. The kiss was soft and chaste – hardly a kiss at all – but just as it ended Lachlan bit her lip.

The promise of something more, if Clara wanted it.

The girl was breathless and rosy-cheeked when Lachlan pulled away. A rush ran through him at the sight of her. "Tell me your last name," he breathed, the order barely audible over the breeze ruffling Clara's hair around her face.

She opened her eyes, parting her lips as if to speak and –

The sound of bells clamoured through the air.

Clara took a step away from Lachlan immediately, eyes bright and wide and entirely lucid once more.

"I have to go," she said, stumbling backwards to pick up her forgotten basket and cloak before darting away from the forest.

No matter, Lachlan thought, as he dropped from the branch to the forest floor. *I shall see her again. I will have her name next time.*

But he was disappointed.

Now he had to go to his mother's funeral alone, with no entertainment to distract him from his grief when evening came.

*

ACKNOWLEDGEMENTS

Another month, another fairy tale retelling. It took me months to finish plotting Tower to get it just the way I wanted it, but I think the time and effort was worth it. Evie and Julian join Scarlett and Adrian, and Elina and Kilian, as another bizarre, perfect couple (even if I do say so myself).

Can you see the pattern to my male protagonist names yet? The next book's male hero is called Lachlan, so I guess I'm stuck writing names ending in "-an" forever. I bet that will be fun a few books down the line.

I'm honestly astounded to be releasing the third book in a series (especially since I still need to release book two in both the Assassin and Monsters trilogy!). And the fourth is on its way! I really enjoy writing these fairy tales. I hope you enjoy reading them too.

I'm not sure who I've had the most fun writing so far in the Curses universe, but Evie and Julian are pretty damn high up on the list. Their dynamic was so much fun! I dithered over making Evie a bubbly, annoying heroine because that's how Rapunzel is portrayed in Tangled, but ultimately I stuck to my guns and love her all the more for it. And of course I'm obsessed with Julian. He's a grumpy 30-year-old grandfather type, after all. What's not to love?

If you couldn't guess from the name Lachlan, the next Curses book, Prince of Foxes, is a Scottish fairy tale! I'm so excited to write a twist on my native Celtic roots for all of you.

As always I'd like to thank my editor, Kirsty; my partner, Jake; my lovely bunnies, and all my readers scattered across the globe. I'd be nothing without you.

Onto the next one!

Hayley

ABOUT THE AUTHOR

Hayley Louise Macfarlane hails from the very tiny hamlet of Balmaha on the shores of Loch Lomond in Scotland. Having spent eight years studying at the University of Glasgow and graduating with a BSc (hons) in Genetics and then a PhD in Synthetic Biology, Hayley quickly realised that her long-term passion for writing trumped her desire to work in a laboratory.

Now Hayley spends her time writing across a whole host of genres. After spending much of 2019 writing fairy tales she'll be branching into apocalyptic science fiction, paranormal & urban fantasy and maybe even a touch of horror in 2020. But never fear: the fairy tales won't be away for long!

During 2019, Hayley set herself the ambitious goal of publishing one thing every month. Seven books, two novellas, two short stories and one box set later, she made it. She recommends that anyone who values their sanity and a sensible sleep cycle does not try this.

Made in the USA
Middletown, DE
25 March 2021

36231220R00175